THE TALLCHIEFS
THE BELOVED, BESTSELLING
MINISERIES BY CAIT LONDON
CONTINUES!

In *The Seduction of Fiona Tallchief,* you'll share
in the love story that has all of Amen Flats,
Wyoming, talking. Because many years ago, the
Tallchief siblings were orphaned by a man named
Palladin. A man whose three innocent sons were
run out of town. And now, the three Palladin
brothers have come home to make their own
peace—and find their own love—with Tallchief
women. In this novel, you'll meet Joel, a strong,
sexy hero you'll never forget!

And coming from Silhouette Desire in
August, be sure to look for the next book in
THE TALLCHIEFS miniseries, when
Rafe Palladin shares his love story. You'll find
a sneak preview of this sensual, emotional
love story waiting for you at the end of
The Seduction of Fiona Tallchief.

Dear Reader,

This month Silhouette Desire brings you six brand-new, emotional and sensual novels by some of the bestselling—and most beloved—authors in the romance genre. Cait London continues her hugely popular miniseries THE TALLCHIEFS with *The Seduction of Fiona Tallchief,* April's MAN OF THE MONTH. Next, Elizabeth Bevarly concludes her BLAME IT ON BOB series with *The Virgin and the Vagabond.* And when a socialite confesses her virginity to a cowboy, she just might be *Taken by a Texan,* in Lass Small's THE KEEPERS OF TEXAS miniseries.

Plus, we have Maureen Child's *Maternity Bride, The Cowboy and the Calendar Girl,* the last in the OPPOSITES ATTRACT series by Nancy Martin, and Kathryn Taylor's tale of domesticating an office-bound hunk in *Taming the Tycoon.*

I hope you enjoy all six of Silhouette Desire's selections this month—and every month!

Regards,

Melissa Senate

Senior Editor
Silhouette Books

Please address questions and book requests to:
Silhouette Reader Service
U.S.: 3010 Walden Ave., P.O. Box 1325, Buffalo, NY 14269
Canadian: P.O. Box 609, Fort Erie, Ont. L2A 5X3

CAIT LONDON
THE SEDUCTION OF FIONA TALLCHIEF

SILHOUETTE *Desire*®
Published by Silhouette Books
America's Publisher of Contemporary Romance

To Tanner Franklin Davis,
born December 21, 1996.

 SILHOUETTE BOOKS

ISBN 0-373-76135-X

THE SEDUCTION OF FIONA TALLCHIEF

Copyright © 1998 by Lois Kleinsasser

This edition published by arrangement with Harlequin Books S.A.

® and TM are trademarks of Harlequin Books S.A., used under license. Trademarks indicated with ® are registered in the United States Patent and Trademark Office, the Canadian Trade Marks Office and in other countries.

Printed in U.S.A.

Books by Cait London

CAIT LONDON

lives in the Missouri Ozarks but loves to travel the Northwest's gold rush/cattle drive trails every summer. She loves research trips, meeting people and going to Native American dances. Ms. London is an avid reader who loves to paint, play with computers and grow herbs—particularly scented geraniums right now. She's a national bestselling and award-winning author, and she also writes historical romances under another pseudonym. Three is her lucky number; she has three daughters, and the events in her life have always been in threes. "I love writing for Silhouette," she says. "One of the best perks about all this hard work is the thrilling reader response and the warm, snug sense that I have given readers an enjoyable, entertaining gift."

Dear Reader,

Thank you for your enthusiastic response to the Tallchief family. From your letters, I see that you love them as much as I do. (I really appreciate those letters.) Duncan, Calum, Elspeth, Birk and Fiona are absolutely dedicated to each other, and the dynamic entrances of their loves enrich this strong family. To my delight as a writer—and reader, I had everything I adore in this family—the West, heritages, legends and, like a cherry on top of a sundae, steamy, evocative romances. At times, there were tears, especially when it was time to leave one story and begin another. Now I invite you to meet the Palladins next, an exciting addition/twist to the Tallchiefs. I had to write about Joel, Rafe and Nick Palladin as they struggle with their dark legacy, which changed the lives of the Tallchiefs. Love doesn't come easy to the Palladin brothers, especially when they tangle with Tallchiefs. Enjoy.

Cait London

To finish the circle, an unlikely love of the battlemaiden will come calling, bearing his angry dragon on one arm and the chest to win her heart. Then the magic circle will be as true as their love.

Prologue

"Good? I just haven't tried to be 'good' yet. It can't be that hard," ten-year-old Fiona snapped at her family. Dressed in her nightgown, she shoved through the kitchen door she had been listening against and stood ramrod straight. She crossed her arms and leveled her stare at her older sister and brothers seated around the kitchen table. "Hold a powwow, a family meeting, in which I'm the problem, will you? And not invite me? What about my rights? Aren't I a Tallchief, same as you? Is that fair?"

Nothing was fair. The cold October night shrouded the Tallchief house the afternoon after Matthew and Pauline Tallchief had been killed. They'd stopped for pizza, a special treat for their five children waiting at their ranch home, and had interrupted a convenience store robbery.

Her brothers had set off immediately on horseback, tracking the killer into the mountains. While Elspeth stayed with Fiona, the Tallchief brothers proved that they had been taught by the best tracker in the country, their father—who had learned the skill from their Sioux great-great-grandfather, Tallchief. The killer's flight into the rugged Rocky Mountain night hadn't saved him.

At dawn, Fiona's brothers had ridden back into Amen Flats, Wyoming, the killer walking behind their horses and tied to a rope.

Her brothers had become men instantly, their boyhood gone, replaced by gaunt, grim shadows of men bound by duty and sadness. Elspeth, her pride holding her chin high and squaring her shoulders, had already set about taking up the task of feeding the family. Fiona wanted to smash something; she wanted to hide in the safety of her father's arms. She wanted her mother to tell her that everything was a bad dream.

She fought back tears and faced Duncan, her eldest brother at eighteen. With the Tallchief height, black, glossy hair, gray eyes and rugged, high cheekbones, he reminded her of her father, and an arrow of pain sliced through her. She couldn't afford not to be strong now, not when they worried about her. "I've got the same black hair from our great-great-grandfather, Tallchief, and our great-great-grandmother's gray Scottish eyes. I know how he captured Una Fearghus and how she was an indentured servant and how they fell in love. And how she sold her dowry to keep Tallchief land safe. That's why we have Tallchief Mountain and our cattle ranch today. I listened when Mother read Una's journals to us. I know how Mom was a judge and how Dad got his tracking skills handed down from his father before him. I know all that. Don't you sit here and plan what to do without me and how to protect me. Don't you dare! I can carry my share."

Duncan looked at his brothers and other sister. At seventeen, Calum nodded. Sixteen-year-old Birk, usually happy and teasing, nodded grimly. Fourteen-year-old Elspeth lifted her chin, and in each of her family, Fiona saw a bit of her parents. Her brothers and Elspeth were dressed in flannel shirts and jeans and boots, which meant they had been out in the cold mountain wind, tending the ranch while she'd selfishly slept, her head tucked beneath her mother's hand-stitched quilt, hoping to awaken and find the nightmare gone.

She hated the man who shot her parents, the fiery emotion pulsed through her, devouring her.

"If you are not very, very good, Fiona—" Duncan began slowly, methodically picking through his thoughts as he looked at the others.

"Be careful," Calum warned. "She's only ten and it's a big weight."

Fiona stared at him. "I'm getting mad. You keep treating me like a kid, and there's no telling what I'll do," she warned quietly.

"She has the right to know what's at stake," Birk stated.

"I'm in. What's the plan? And can we pull it off?" Fiona flipped back her long black braids and leaned on the table with her hands. She looked at her family, read their sorrow and grim determination. She saw Duncan the defender, Calum the cool, Birk the rogue and Elspeth the elegant. The play names suited them and they were hers now, more than ever.

A wash of October leaves, tossed by the wind, slashed against the window as she leveled a look at each one. They needed her. With her in the plan, the Tallchiefs could do anything.

"Agreed," Elspeth added after a slow look around the table.

"There will be people watching us," Duncan began slowly. "We'll have to mind our business—"

"Or?" Fiona shot back. "Just what is our business?" Wasn't her business living and playing with the barn cats, leaping into the stacked hay and riding her bicycle and tormenting her brothers and—

One look at her family told her that with two bullets, the world had flopped over and crushed her life.

Calum leveled a look at Fiona. "Our business is to stay together, and it starts tomorrow, when people start calling and visiting and bringing over tears and casseroles. Then there's the funeral, and we're putting Mom and Dad on the mountain to sleep. But the five of us have to look as if we're staying together from the start."

Elspeth flicked her brothers a look and sighed. "*They* can't handle crying women. That's up to us, Fiona."

"Right. Crying, sobbing, wailing, tear-dripping women bearing tuna and rice casseroles. I can handle them." But could she handle the fear and the sorrow within herself?

She would. Her brothers and sister would tell her what to do, and she would do it. *Mom? Dad? Please come home? I'm scared!*

Calum tapped his pencil on the pad in front of him. Birk looked at Duncan, and Duncan looked at Elspeth.

Fiona shivered. "You're worried they'll try to take me away, aren't you?"

She fought the icy fear surging through her, curling her hands into fists. She shivered, willing her mother to come hold her. How could her mother's kitchen, still fragrant from applesauce cake, and the pantry, lined with jars of her best jams, be so empty? *Mom? Dad?*

"They won't take you away," Duncan said quietly, drawing her onto his lap. "Because you'll be so good, they'll all see how well you're doing and how happy you are."

Fiona burrowed closer to him. "Just how good?" she asked very cautiously.

"No causes," Elspeth stated. "No leading the rebels."

"Before you leap into any right-versus-wrong battles or fight for the underdog, you have to tell us about it," Birk added. "We'll decide—together—if you need to take action, or if we can help."

"Just who is going to take care of the bullies of the world? They have to be stopped, you know," Fiona demanded, outraged that she was asked to desert the defenseless.

"You will. When you grow up," Calum said, lifting her onto his lap and holding her. "And you're going to have very good grades in all your subjects. If you need help—"

Fiona hugged Calum. He smelled of wood smoke and leather and cattle and of love. She looked around the table at her family. They needed her.

"Aye," she stated, using the Tallchiefs' word to swear upon their honor. "I'll be a perfect little angel," Fiona the fiery vowed and then began to cry as she moved onto Birk's lap, and Elspeth's arms curled around them.

Mom? Dad?

One

"**G**et off Tallchief Mountain. It's *my* mountain," Joel murmured, repeating what a ten-year-old girl had yelled at him twenty years earlier. Fiona Tallchief's fierce challenge rang in his mind as though it were yesterday.

Joel glanced at his knuckles, recently skinned in a brawl. He skimmed his hand expertly over the classic sports car's steering wheel, guiding it around a sharp mountain curve. Bright red, white and easily noticed, the 1958 Corvette convertible seemed perfect for what he wanted to do—dive right into the nest of Tallchiefs in Amen Flats, Wyoming, and face his past. At thirty-seven and a corporate attorney for his grandmother's company, Joel Palladin knew how to make dramatic statements.

The first week of October lay cold and black on the Rocky Mountains, reminding him of the day he and his brothers, Nick and Rafe, had come to the Tallchiefs' funeral. Cramped and dirty from the bus trip from Denver, they'd arrived too late for the church service. They had spent their last "eating money" renting horses for the second private service high on Tallchief Mountain. They were city boys, tough and wary, yet grimly determined to complete their mission in the cliffs, meadows and wild forests of Tallchief Mountain. Their father had left them little honor, but the scrap that remained demanded that they apologize for him.

Joel glanced in the rearview mirror. Though he hadn't had time to shave, and a new stubble covered his jaw, he found the dark skin and hard features of his father stamped upon him. Lloyd Palladin had left his mark on his three sons—the same jutting cheekbones, soaring dark brown brows over deep-set, green eyes, a prominent jaw and a cleft in his chin. While Lloyd had let his unsavory passions rule him, the three grown Palladin sons kept a firm rein on their pride and their emotions. Nick, Rafe and Joel were painfully aware of their dark legacy and their inability to deal with softer emotions.

Joel inhaled sharply at the memory of his father's open hand connecting with his mother's cheek. As a child he could do little to protect her, and as a man he feared that Lloyd's wild passions could one day be his own. He feared coming too close to emotions, controlling himself even during sex. A big, powerful man, Joel could easily hurt a woman—

He did not want to hurt Fiona Tallchief, but he needed to reckon with his unexpected desire and fascination for her.

That day twenty years ago lay fresh in Joel's mind as he expertly handled the small sports car he'd purchased a few days ago. Lost in his thoughts as he sped toward the old homestead he had acquired, Joel saw the animal too late to stop. He expertly swerved around the deer poised in his headlights and prayed that the animal wouldn't leap the wrong way. The doe safely bounded off into the woods.

Joel flicked on his sound system, settling down with Mozart and his thoughts, accustomed to staying on track in emergencies. After a long, hard, tense week fighting his grandmother's corporate battles and his rebellious son, Joel didn't want to be pushed by anyone. He ran his finger over the long knife-cut in the convertible's vinyl top, which he'd temporarily patched with duct tape. Caught in the act of stripping and stealing his newly purchased Corvette, the gang that had jumped him in the alley soon discovered that he was in no mood for orders.

Fiona Tallchief had started issuing orders to him when she was ten, and again two years ago when she was twenty-eight. The hot tirade coming from her mouth while he stood covered in sludge had almost caused him to lose control. "Iron Man Palladin" let very few issues disrupt his cool and few women interrupt his sleep. When something nettled him—and hot-blooded, lean and leggy Fiona Tallchief did—Joel took action. An emotional, volatile woman, she wouldn't fit into his streamlined life on a permanent basis, yet Fiona excited him on a primitive level, igniting desire that had surprised and bothered him. That raw desire caused him to be uneasy; he sensed Fiona Tallchief could test his control, and he didn't like that feeling. In a bold move typical for him, he intended to settle two mismatched corners of his life: Cody, his troubled ten-year-old son and Fiona Tallchief.

Dressed in his favorite battered leather jacket that had taken his first paycheck to buy, years ago, a biker's club T-shirt, black jeans and boots, Joel rolled his shoulders and settled his six-foot-four frame more comfortably into the plush, low seat, preparing for the long drive to the ranch he had just purchased.

Though he had not seen it, the old homestead was not far from Amen Flats, within bicycle riding distance, and Cody needed— Well, what Cody needed, Joel had decided, was a firm hand and love. Mamie, Joel's grandmother, was temporarily taking charge of those duties. Mamie was providing a buffer for the transition between Cody's mother's negligence and Joel, who was about to become an active parent. Cody was Joel's son and his responsibility. Buying the run-down ranch was a long shot; Joel hoped that Cody would take pride in bringing it to life.

Trying to get closer to his surly son at this stage was a long shot, but Joel was determined. He held few illusions about the trail that Cody appeared to be taking. Joel's ex-wife, Cody's mother, had walked away from her son to a new husband. Cody had settled in to fight the world with older, wiser boys.

Joel glanced down at his recently dirtied, torn clothing. He preferred to travel in his comfortable clothing, but the scuffle with the gang had added dirt and grease. As a toddler he had learned how to fight, and now, at thirty-seven, he felt as cold and hard as steel. Except with Cody.

He'd badly failed his son, and Cody was on his way to a path Joel had already traveled.

A temporary relocation in Amen Flats wasn't the answer, but it was a start. He glanced at the flashy hubcaps in the tiny back seat. He'd interrupted the gang just as they'd begun stripping his car and had already cut open the top with a knife. No one ever took anything from Joel, until he was ready to give it. Along the way he'd made a few enemies but nothing serious, and now the gun on the seat beside him would provide protection if he needed it in his new home.

He wiped his hand across the dark stubble covering his jaw, resenting the lack of sleep and time. The rectangular rearview mirror reflected the image of a hardened, dangerous man. Meticulous, suit-clad attorney Joel Palladin had been left in another state.

Joel inhaled grimly and settled down in the leather seat. He was too tired to be driving, and yet he couldn't rest.

He hadn't slept in years, not deeply, fully: the ten-year-old girl's fierce tear-filled expression had haunted him relentlessly. Because of his robbery of the convenience store, Lloyd Palladin had left five youths without parents, eight including his sons.

Amen Flats. The Tallchiefs. Fiona Tallchief, the girl; wild temper raging as fierce as the mountain winds, ordering him off her mountain.

The Fiona Tallchief of two years ago strolled back into his mind: that lean, taut feminine body—the woman, a rebel hurrying through life. She was incensed that Palladin, Inc. was bulldozing over a pond filled with tiny, helpless frogs and a unique ecosystem. Before he could rise from his desk, she'd hefted a bucket filled with sludge from the frog pond and dumped it over his head.

She'd haunted him, and Joel sensed his destiny lay in facing the rip in the Tallchiefs' lives that his father had created. Was it wrong to bring his son into the past?

Why did Fiona Tallchief, the girl and the woman, haunt him? Why did she fascinate him enough that he kept clippings of her causes in several states? She'd been too quiet for months, nestling in the safety of the Tallchief family. *Quiet* wasn't in Fiona's vocabulary—her quotes in newspapers were like spears jabbed at slumlords, poorly run government programs and "spoiled dese-craters of the environment," a term she had used for Joel as she had dumped the sludge on his most expensive, custom-tailored, pin-striped suit with matching vest.

A man who had climbed out of the slums, Joel appreciated fine clothing. His Armani shirt and tie had been ruined, his custom-made shoes—

Joel narrowed his eyes, concentrating on the curving road. That same convenience store lay ahead.

"Elephants and eighteen-wheelers and lonely Rocky Mountain roads at one o'clock in the morning...how much more can a girl ask for?" Fiona spoke into the microphone attached to her sweat-shirt and geared down the truck. "Coming into a curve, Eunice," she said into the speaker which led to another in the trailer section of the rig. "Brace yourself."

The companion loudspeaker on her dashboard made smushy, sniffy noises, which said that Eunice's snout was investigating the speaker. Fiona smiled grimly at the reassuring noise. "There is no way that zoo is going to sell you to someone who isn't prepared to take care of you. Trust me, baby. I've been in these battles before, and I'm no lightweight. I'll keep you safe from harm while I raise a stink about Timba Simba Land's animal neglect. The zoo wouldn't dare complete the sale to TS Land. I do not care if you are undersized and the zoo wants to display a normal-sized elephant. I'll strangle their donations to zero and have the reporters at their doorstep. Meanwhile, you'll be safe."

Just one last cause, then she would settle quietly to her florist shop, Hummingbirds. She jammed her trucker's boot against the clutch and shifted easily. At five foot ten, she fit comfortably into the padded seat. She narrowed her eyes on the road in front of her, lit by the truck's lights. "All I have to do is find a place to keep you. It's a small matter. Amen Flats—we're in Wyoming now, baby—is where I grew up. I've got family and friends who will all help me, but I'd prefer not to endanger them. We'll be just fine. I'll tuck you in some nice barn with plenty of food.

We'll eat peanuts and talk girl talk. I'll do your toenails and give you a beauty bath.''

She patted the book on the seat beside her. *Simple Everyday Elephant Care* was a manual every flower shop and greenhouse owner should have, right along with flower bulb care. "Aye," she said, continuing to talk because the sound settled Eunice. "I thought I was tough, and then just after the funeral, I found I wasn't. It was just twenty years ago and a cold October when we laid my parents on the mountain.''

Fiona shifted down again as the curve wound downward, and then shifted again to make another curve, leading upward through the pines. "Duncan was only eighteen, but ready to take responsibility for everything—us, the ranch, everything. He had a plan to 'put the glue' in our sticking together, he said. By that time, I knew that my parents weren't coming home—Mom to make dinner and to weave and to read us stories from Una's journals. Dad to work with the sheep and the cattle and to hold me on his lap. Within hours after they were killed, I knew that one wrong move from me could tear our family apart, and I was scared...oh, so scared. Out at Tallchief Lake in the storm with Duncan holding me on his hip and Calum and Birk and Elspeth close by, we each pledged to return a portion of Una's dowry to the Tallchiefs. We raised our thumbs to the night sky—we've all got scars to prove that we've taken our vows to stay together. We shouted 'Aye!' to that hard, cold wind and pledged to do our best.''

Fiona shivered, scanning the aspens and pines along the road as she came closer to the small taillights ahead of her. "I said I'd be good, Eunice, and I was. I'd always been fascinated by the stories of Una's sewing chest and by its legend. Tallchief thought that he'd have her easily, and when he first found that the conquest wasn't that easy, he crafted her a horsehair bracelet and a ring, decorated in small, sky blue beads. She wouldn't wear them unless he wore a matching set, and after a blazing argument, he wore those she had crafted for him. They were mistakenly left in the small sewing chest with sewing things and Celtic jewelry, and it was lost. The legend that accompanies the chest is lovely, but I was always too busy to really hunt for the chest. Being good takes full-time energy, you know.''

Eunice's continued muffled, exploring sounds were pleasant and companionable in the night.

"We're coming into a straight stretch soon, not too far from Amen Flats. Elspeth is married to Alek Petrovna and Calum to Alek's sister, Talia. Birk and Lacy are fixing up that old bordello, and Duncan and Sybil are living in the old place. Duncan added onto it, of course. Emily, Sybil's teenage daughter, and their daughter, Megan, and son, Daniel, live there, too. My older brothers were always protecting us, and Elspeth detested it. The Black Knights are keeping busy now, changing diapers. Elspeth has found what she's needed in Alek and their baby. When things cool down, I'd like you to meet them, Eunice."

Fiona gripped the huge wheel. Danny Marbles, an activist like herself, had given her a quick course in driving trucks and had loaned her a top-performing burgundy Mack with artistic scroll-work on the hood and sides. A row of cab lights ran across the top between twin highly polished, vertical exhaust pipes. The rig—a fancy steel grill on the cab and the semitrailer—had a luxurious sleeper cab just behind the front seat. Danny had said he wanted Eunice transported in style and had gifted Fiona with a sweatshirt that read "Tallchief's Pachyderm Express."

Truckers' logbooks weren't a problem. Danny had laid a path straight from Missouri to Amen Flats that bypassed the check-points.

Fiona studied the small taillights that she had just come upon. "Eunice, there's a small sports car ahead of me, and he's not letting me get a run at the hills. I can't pass him right now to pick up speed for the next hill, and he's not making me happy. I'd blow the air horn at him, but Danny is right...we have to keep low-key on this right now, until you're safe. All we need is some spoiled jerk turning us in to the law. Once Danny knows you're safe, he'll start revving up the press. Jerk! Not you, Eunice— him," Fiona stated as the small car took its share of the road, not allowing her to pass and then kept its speed even, not allowing her to pick up speed on the downhill run.

She shifted repeatedly, gearing for the steep uphill grade. The truck crawled upward, burdened by Eunice's weight. "Whoever taught that guy road etiquette needed a brain. Probably one of those spoiled sons of the wealthy," she stated into the microphone pinned to her collar. She had stolen a Missouri elephant; she had driven across Kansas on back roads and reached Wyoming, all within twenty-four hours. She hadn't slept and she wasn't in the mood for expensive sports cars or ill-mannered drivers. She began to pass the car on a straight stretch, and it swerved to the center, preventing her move.

"Fine. Have it your way, buddy," she said, and settled down to control her simmering mood. She couldn't afford to be in a hurry and make mistakes, not with Eunice in her keeping.

She'd kept her temper and shoved her causes into a back drawer more than once when she was growing up. The weight of the Tallchiefs' survival as a family sometimes seemed to balance on her shoulders; child welfare agencies were always close, watching. Fiona tried not to look at the small convenience store, neon lights blazing, at the side of the road. Her parents had stopped for pizza that night at the same place—

She inhaled, glancing at the store. A flash of metal caught her attention, and she slowed the truck. Through the windows, she saw the clerk's hands raised and two men, faces hidden in ski masks, holding sawed-off shotguns.

Mom? Dad?

Fiona closed her eyes as pain and bitterness slashed through her. She knew what she had to do. "Sorry, Eunice. We've just come upon a bit of a small delay. That fancy little sports car is going to have to go on without us for a while," she said as she quickly used the jake brake and slowed the truck.

Joel Palladin glanced in his rearview mirror. The eighteen-wheeler that had been too close to Joel's expensive back bumper was slowing down. The big rig slowly turned around on the highway, headlamps cutting into the roadside pines. The driver must have needed gas or a rest stop.

Joel had been too busy as an attorney, protecting his grandmother's powerful corporation in Denver, to see how badly Cody needed him. Joel curled his fingers around the Corvette's steering wheel and frowned. He'd never been a part of his son's life; Patrice had seen to that. His times with his son had been uncomfortable, despite Joel's efforts to communicate. He should have sensed the boy's need from Cody's refusal to talk with him or to see him. He remembered how he'd been just like his son once: rebellious, ready to fight, and cocky. Cody had been too proud to tell his father that he'd been staying untended in his mother's old apartment for months.

Joel knew about being a neglected child. His paternal grandmother, Mamie Palladin, was half his size and weight and twice as tough. After she'd taken on the raising of Joel and his brothers, Rafe and Nick, she had methodically dissected their teenage hardcase attitudes and put them back together with love.

Cody wasn't the only reason Joel wanted to settle near Amen Flats, Wyoming. He had an old debt to settle and a firewoman to hunt. This time, hot-tempered dynamo Fiona Tallchief wouldn't have the protection of Joel's grandmother, and the battle would be one-on-one.

The fancy cab lights of the truck behind him turned, catching Joel's attention as the rig was poised at an odd angle to the road.

"He's ramming the store!" Joel muttered and expertly geared down. With the ease of a man who raced cars and knew them well, Joel didn't stop: he braked and spun the steering wheel causing the car to do a one-eighty and face in the other direction. He shifted down for power and the motor surged to life. The tires squealed, as the high-powered car ate up the highway to the store.

The truck smashed through the front of the brightly lit store just as Joel's car screeched to a stop. Glistening sheets of glass speared into the night and shards fell like rain down around the truck's cab.

In a heartbeat, Joel recognized the scene in front of him. The two men, big ones, in ski masks, denim jackets and dirty jeans, held sawed-off shotguns at a male clerk, who looked terrified. The robbers had handguns tucked into their belts. At the side of the building, a fast Chevy waited, motor running. The trucker, no more than a boy wearing a ball cap and sweatshirt and jeans, had slid from the passenger side of the cab and crouched, circling the Mack's hood.

"A little abrupt and expensive, but serving the purpose," Joel muttered as he reached to the seat beside him. Without looking, he grabbed the automatic gun and slammed the clip he'd previously removed into the butt, loading it. He ducked as a bullet hissed by his head and a man's rough curse carried over the Mack's purring motor. Moving quickly, Joel circled the slender trucker, who dove to the floor at the sound of a second shot. The robbers weren't going anywhere quickly. The Mack was taking up the whole front of the store and now, at the rear exit, Joel had a special dislike for convenience store holdups.

"Get down!" Joel yelled to the trucker, who glanced at him over his shoulder. A boy, Joel thought, sizing up the slender five-foot-ten build and the pale oval face beneath the ball cap. The youth was too young to die, but smart enough to get himself in real trouble. The robbers had discarded the empty shotguns and were wildly firing their handguns at Joel while he came closer.

In a heartbeat the trucker braced one hand on a low shelf and vaulted over it. He headed toward the men, carrying a broom like a spear.

"Crazy...!" Joel had to distract them, or the trucker was dead. Just as the men leveled their weapons at the trucker, Joel stood, attracting their attention again and fired over their heads, sending canned spinach tumbling down around them. He leaped behind tall, stacked displays of disposable diapers and big cans of fruit juice. The cardboard man advertising the diapers grinned at him. "Shut up," Joel muttered and stepped out from the display.

While the thieves dodged the torrent of cans, and the trucker rammed them with the broom, Joel had his own problem. The tower of fruit juice cans came down on him and the world went black. Joel crumpled in a sea of fragrant disposable diapers.

He fought to the painful surface and recognized the warm, sticky feel of his blood running down his temple. A woman stood over him, long legs spread, her hands on her waist as she studied him.

Diamonds glittered on her shoulders, and whoever she was, Joel wanted her. While his head throbbed painfully, her blurred face looked down at him as if she were a goddess regarding and disdaining a mere mortal. There was strength in her face, a blurred oval image of black, winged brows and smoky eyes and a full mouth with an odd, tantalizing lift to one side. She was almost boyishly lean, and in that heartbeat, he knew that their lives were intertwined, that she was a part of him. He would treat her like a goddess, take care of her, protect her. She would be his, and the emptiness would end. He'd been hunting for this woman all his life, and now she couldn't get away. He managed to grip her booted ankle. If she left him now, he might never find her. "Don't leave me. I can't stay here," he managed and added mentally, *without you.*

She stood over him. And for Joel, time stretched from heartbeats to millenniums as she considered him. Finally she dusted the diamonds from her shoulders and tugged up her leather gloves. "He's mine," she said firmly in a voice that claimed him from the darkness, a voice he would never forget.

He felt himself being lifted and the woman's low sultry voice repeated in the distance. "Aye," she said slowly, firmly, as though making a promise to herself. "He's mine. I'm taking him."

The woman's husky voice continued to talk, a steady hum covered by the pain spearing inside Joel's head. The bed swayed continuously beneath him, and he forced his hand to grab at whatever was brushing his face. Holding it at bay, he forced open his lids to see a lacy bra.

On the other side of the curtains, the woman continued talking, as Joel warily took in his surroundings, inhaling the fresh, delicate scent of a woman—like a mountain wind brushing the tops of bluebells and daisies. He was stretched out in the sleeper cab of a truck, an array of lacy, feminine underwear drying on a line over his head. He remembered being shoved and pushed and cursed at by the woman determined to save him. At one point, trying to fit him into the cab, she'd grabbed his belt and helped hoist him. While he'd felt like a sack of bruised potatoes, she'd been telling the two truckers who had lifted Joel into the cab how she didn't like being called "Sweet Honey" and "Baby Doll." In no uncertain terms she'd told them that she was no "babe" and not their "baby."

"I know, Eunice." Her crooning tone was sultry, musical, low and vaguely familiar. "But whatever he's done, I couldn't leave him to face the law. He did come back to help us. Before we left, I made certain that the clerk had everything under control. The thieves were bound on the floor, the call was in to the sheriff's department, and the clerk said he could handle the wait. But we have to hide this rig fast, and I don't have a clue where."

Joel waited. Eunice did not answer, despite the questions the woman shoved at her.

Fine. His frown started the hammer pounding in his head. Eunice, in addition to ramming convenience stores with an eighteen-wheeler, talked to herself. Joel eased the bag from beside his head, and peanuts slid from it. The crinkly sound around his ears stopped when he removed the disposable diaper used to cover the two bloody cuts on his forehead. He listened to the excited chatter on the truck's citizens' band radio—the sheriff investigating a convenience store robbery.

"We've got you covered, baby doll," a trucker's raw, deep tone cut into the woman's steady talk. "Don't worry about a thing, sweet thing. You got any idea where you're goin'?"

"Oh, fine, Eunice," the woman muttered quietly. "The big boys rescuing little old helpless me." After the click of a microphone, she said, "I'm working on it. Thanks."

"Anytime, sugar," the trucker drawled.

Another trucker cut in to correct and to give Fiona a CB name. "Beefcake, the lady doesn't like being called sugar. She's a lady, okay? Warrior Lady is her handle. Anytime you talk to her, you use that name, got it?"

The woman continued to talk now, quietly, steadily, as if to herself. "Oh, fine. Just fine. Now we're in a convoy, Eunice. Three trucks ahead of us and three behind. So much for being inconspicuous. So much for taking back roads and letting you exercise in hidden valleys and deserted barns. Don't think that you're the cause of this problem. There was no way I was ignoring that robbery. And you know me, I'm a woman who takes action—"

"Breaker. Truckers, this is the sheriff." While the man spoke over the radio, the muffled sounds of opera sopranos trilled in the background. "I'm looking for a big rig. Burgundy, fancy grill, lights across the top. He's just smashed into a convenience store and stopped a robbery in progress. A big, tough-looking guy helped, was injured, and the trucker hauled him off. Come back?'' he asked, requesting an answer.

Joel glanced at the clock fastened above his head. Forty-five minutes had passed since he'd dropped into the trucker's war against the thieves. He noted his gun—minus the bullet clip— tossed into an opened canvas backpack. He eased it from the cluttered rainbow of lacy lingerie and gingerly stuck it into his belt.

The truckers were protectively quiet. ''Aye and blast,'' the woman cursed. ''Sorry, Eunice. I didn't mean to say that. I reserve it for when I really mean it.''

''No big burgundy rig on the roads this morning, Sheriff,'' one of the truckers stated over the sounds of Elvis Presley.

''I know you're awake,''·the woman said over her shoulder to Joel. ''You might as well come sit up front. I want you out of my rig as soon as you think you're able. There's a thermos of hot coffee up here, courtesy of the store clerk, and some packaged sandwiches. In fact, there's three grocery sacks up here that he filled, and more diapers for your head. Has the bleeding stopped?''

Joel's stomach rose as the truck rounded a curve. He sat slowly and touched his head. He patted the cuts gingerly with a fresh diaper. ''I'm okay.''

He was badly bruised, had a headache the size of the Mack and felt woozy. Or was the scent of the woman who geared the truck in swift, competent and irritated movements causing him to feel light-headed? He took a deep breath and moved carefully into the passenger's seat, tossing the *Simple Everyday Elephant Care* book into the sleeper and easing his feet around the grocery bags on the floor.

''It's almost three o'clock in the morning, and I could use a cup of coffee. Pour one for me, okay? Now, listen up. I do not have time to spend on a car thief, nor can I become involved in your problems. I do not care why you are running from the law and hot-wired that fast little number. I do not care if your children need braces and your wife has left you and your brother needs another sterilization because the first one didn't work and he has ten kids. I just do not care," she underlined firmly. "Just get your sizable self out whenever you can stand and drive. It was no easy job packing your weight into the cab. I had to have help. That expensive toy you stole is rigged to the back of my trailer. And do not try anything funny. I'm not in the mood," she added grimly as Joel began to pour coffee.

"You're a mouthy little thing. What makes you think I stole the car?" Because he needed coffee more than air at the moment, he sipped the hot brew, feeling it revive him. He took a quick inventory of his bruised body and decided he'd live.

She expertly shifted for a long hill, then tossed him a bottle of aspirin from the cluttered dash. "Your outfit doesn't match the money the car would cost, and that is an expensive Dirty Harry gun, and you know how to handle yourself in a robbery situation. You knew to cover the back exit and to distract the men from firing at me. I'd say you've been on the other end of the situation at some time, and whatever it was, I don't care, because you did save my life. I couldn't leave you. Someone else can allow you to go to jail. You saved my life. I was too—angry to have good sense. So that is that."

Joel swallowed the aspirin and poured a second cup, handing it to her. He paused and inhaled sharply, for in the light of the dashboard and the moonlight coming in through the truck's windows, was Fiona Tallchief.

Two

Joel's heart kicked up into overdrive, and he forced his hand not to tremble, locking it to his tense thigh. He'd been tracking Miss Fiona Tallchief through the press for years, keeping tabs on her, and now she sat within reach. He skimmed the features beneath her ball cap, the flashing eyes that had reminded him of steel wrapped in smoke, the long silky lashes without cosmetics and the firm, somewhat sharp line of her chin, giving her face an elfin look. The striking contrast had set him simmering. There was no way he could forget her mouth, though the last time he'd seen her, she'd been stalking back and forth across his office and ripping him apart: "You money-hungry, spoiled, brand-name-toting capitalist, fed by the suffering of our ecosystem. Wear this and see how you like it!" had preceded the bucket of sludge.

Though she was now dressed in a loose sweatshirt and jeans, there was no mistaking that long, lean, taut body. Two years ago, she'd been dressed in a conservative, gray suit. The slit in the skirt had opened as she'd stalked, revealing endless legs. Joel's secretary in the outer office hadn't been able to stop her—when aroused, Fiona Tallchief was an army of one, plowing through any defenses. .

She wouldn't recognize him now, of course. He'd been wearing her bucket of sludge over his head and down his expensive suit.

Joel had wanted to wrap both fists in that long, glossy hair swaying down her back and fuse his mouth to hers. In the light of the truck's dashboard, he traced the uneven, short, boy cut that framed her unique, high-boned cheeks and winged eyebrows. The longer wisps sliding down her neck emphasized the slender column that he knew he could circle with one hand. The uneven lengths of hair fluttered in the warm air coming from the heater, looking like soft, black, glossy feathers. "Did you cut your hair yourself?"

Fiona flicked an impatient glance at him. "I don't have time for chitchat or your problems. If you need a hospital, I'll pull over and one of the truckers will take you."

"You're an independent, competent lady on the move, with no time for anything but exactly what suits you," he murmured, remembering how quickly Fiona became involved with issues that caught her attention. She moved through life at warp speed, never at a loss for a male companion.

She glanced at him impatiently and geared down for another curve. "Think of it this way, buddy. You're in my space and as welcome as three-day-old dead fish in the tropics. Got it? Now, those truckers will remove you forcibly if I want—"

Joel locked his jaw, the muscles tightening, sending a shaft of pain straight into his head. No one was prying him away from Fiona Tallchief, not when fate had dropped her into his hands. But Joel knew her weaknesses very well; he'd studied her for years. Though she shielded her private emotions, a single glittering tear on Fiona's news photograph had captivated him. A tender smile while she'd held a baby had touched Joel's hardened emotions. She was like a warm, magic crystal, shooting off a myriad of color and leaving him waiting for more. *Oh, hell, he admitted reluctantly, she'd enchanted him for years, tantalized him, ruined him for other women.* He laid his head back against the headrest and groaned slightly, just enough to catch her attention.

"I knew it. You've probably got a concussion. Seeing double?'' she asked worriedly and held up two fingers in front of his face. ''How many?''

''Four,'' he lied, and tried another groan, which echoed painfully in his head. To the toughened Palladin brothers, a man who groaned was a sissy. Joel had a quick image of Rafe and Nick sneering.

''Oh, aye and blast. You're sick,'' she muttered darkly. ''I'm stuck with you.'' She shoved her palm against his cheek and jerked it away. ''Aye and blast! You're hot with fever. Maybe one of the truckers could take you off my hands?'' The question was a desperate plea.

He would like Fiona Tallchief to be desperate, wary and needing something from him. ''I don't think I can move,'' he said, meaning it.

A fighter, fighting duty, she tried again, as he knew she would. ''Look, whoever you are. I'm in a fix. I really don't care to chat with the law right now, and if you're wanted for hot-wiring that toy, I can't afford to keep you.''

Keep him? Like a pet? Joel inhaled slowly, holding his temper. He'd never asked a woman to keep him, care for him, but he wanted Fiona within sight. *You'll keep me. I know exactly which buttons to push. I'm very good at solid, logical thinking.* He groaned again and flopped his hand down on the seat. He wasn't entirely acting; Joel had a headache the size of Manhattan, ached from bruises from the gang and the cans, and he badly needed sleep.

Fiona's gloved hand squeezed his. ''You'll be fine. I'll take care of you. They won't get you.''

''They will,'' he murmured, tossing bait to his prey. Once Fiona adopted a cause, a person, nothing could stop her from protecting them. Meanwhile, he had her within his grasp.

''You are with the best, buddy,'' she stated confidently and patted his knee. ''I've done this before.''

''Really?'' he asked, prodding her. Joel quickly calculated that Fiona had been arrested for demonstrations in at least four states. When she believed in a cause, she was fearless and impressive. ''Are you on the lam, too?'' he asked.

She stiffened and clamped her lips closed, and Joel knew he

was right. Fiona had been living quietly in Amen Flats, surrounded by the Tallchiefs' growing family, but now she was on the move again and standing up for an issue in which she believed deeply. The first article he'd read about her was when she was nineteen and embroiled in a protest with a slumlord. With computer access to news articles, Joel had found it easy to trace Fiona.

She squeezed his hand. "I'll take care of you. A hospital would be the first place they'd look. But I've got other...problems."

"Like what?"

Fiona released his hand and concentrated on sailing around a tight curve. "I need a barn, okay? A good one that's nice and warm and has available water. A big one. That way I can park this rig in it and—"

"I know of a place not far from here," Joel offered quietly as he placed his hand to his throbbing head. "It's mine. About a quarter of a mile, and down that lane. You're welcome to use it."

"Oh, right." Her hand slid to smooth his head, a comforting gesture. "Your hideout, right? The old Watkins place, isn't it? All run-down and isolated and that big barn—that big lovely, sweet, accommodating barn with inside water," she exclaimed in the tone of a thirsty person discovering a desert oasis.

She stared at him. "Don't tell me. You've stashed stolen cars in the barn and run a car resale ring. You've got extra used parts in the sports car's back seat, some new parts, and that isn't an average road toolbox."

"I don't think you have any choice but to accept the offer," Joel stated smoothly, covering the flash of temper her accusation aroused. He'd learned at an early age to carry a well-stocked toolbox, and he couldn't wait to tinker with the old pump—a therapy that soothed him.

"Mister, I have always had a lot of choices," she shot back. "By the way, I don't like guns. I threw your gun clip away several miles back."

"That was an expensive statement. Take the offer of my barn or leave it," he returned carelessly, despite the tension running through him. An intuitive, elemental heat skittered around Joel's body. He loved the look of Fiona Tallchief now, all revved up, determined, color high, ready to fight for any cause. He wanted her to want him as desperately as she wanted his barn. He held the deed to his "hideout" and he wanted to get very close to the woman who had haunted him for years.

"At least you're not using this barn to strip stolen cars, reselling the parts or painting and changing the indentification numbers on them," Fiona said, looking around the barn as she helped Joel out of the cab. "It's a shame you cut the top of this convertible, but that's an easy way to steal it. I'll help you into the house and then I'll come back to…ah, bring in the groceries and my things. It's a good thing the entire rig and your stolen car fit into the barn with room to spare. The Watkins built the barn to keep all their stock in during bad winters— Hold on…I'll help you. I've got brothers who are as big as you are, and I've managed them, before and after a brawl."

We've got that in common, Joel thought, remembering the times he had to tend Nick and Rafe. He studied her hands on his chest— slender, pale, capable—and knew that he didn't want her touching another man.

She glanced at the chestnut gelding in the stall and flicked a suspicious look at Joel. "I do not steal horses," he stated tightly. "Meet Dante, and I've got a bill of sale in my pocket."

"One just never knows when one will have to use a mountain trail for a getaway, does one? And a horse would definitely make the difference," she murmured, and glanced at the big gold watch on his wrist. "That's a classy watch you're wearing, very pricey for a guy dressed like you."

"I earned it," he stated grimly. The watch was his reward to himself, a man who worked very hard to succeed. "I've got suits that cost more than you make in a year," he muttered, defending his favorite leather jacket.

"Sure. I believe you, Cinderella," she returned, unimpressed, her tone disbelieving as she glanced around the barn.

"Wrong sex," he managed, amazed that despite his bruises and light-headed feeling, he was still very aware of her soft breast against his side. It was too soft, as if she wasn't wearing a bra. Joel closed his eyes, clamping down on the quick rise of desire. He allowed himself to lean on Fiona, enjoying her arm around him. He draped his arm around her shoulders, focusing on her slender hand taking his. Strength lay in it; a woman who was used to physical work.

She glanced down at his stomach, to the gun stuck in his belt. "I'd prefer you put that away, and in case you have another gun clip, I'd really prefer you didn't have a shoot-out while I'm with you, okay?"

"I'll try not to," he murmured, standing in the cold wind as Fiona turned to shut the big double doors on the barn. She returned to support him, and they moved into the house.

"You've got a key?" she asked, as he opened the door to the darkened house. "Don't tell me where you found it. I don't want to know."

Joel surveyed around the barren, dusty old house. He'd purchased the house unseen, and this was his first view of it. This was what he wanted for Cody, a place to call home, to build together, to belong. The old house felt like home already, despite the lack of water and electricity. Rooms angled off the large living room: a big farm kitchen at one end and several bedrooms. A wall in the sunroom was covered with shelves. In the living room a wood cookstove stood where a heating stove should be, and Joel fell in love with the house instantly, wanting to clean and polish it.

"I used to come here for Mrs. Watkins' apple cobbler," Fiona murmured, glancing around the old house. "She needed me almost as much as I needed her. Her husband had died, and she was trying to manage this place and failing. I had to be 'good,' you see, and I didn't want to tell my brothers and sister how—"

Fiona stiffened beneath Joel's arm. "There was a time when I was so scared that I'd do something wrong and ruin our family."

"That's rough. But I know what you mean." Joel thought back to when he was Rafe and Nick's protector and stealing food to feed them. He was only fourteen when he was first brought before the judge for hot-wiring cars. Fiona was right. He was experienced in theft...and the aftermath of survival that faced Lloyd Palladin's sons.

Joel had the unique experience of Fiona Tallchief gently depositing him in the huge, old, pioneer bed in the living room. The bed was a solid walnut affair, topped by a new, plastic-covered mattress set. Amen Flats Furniture had found the right house and deposited the order he had given by telephone.

"All the comforts. You must be planning to use this place as a base for your operations," Fiona said as she moved quickly to the old cookstove at one end of the living room, crushed a paper sack and stuffed it into the stove. She expertly adjusted the damper and placed kindling and wood on the paper. One strike of the match lit the fire, and she glanced at him over her shoulder. "Lie still. I'll only be gone for a minute."

After she lit a thick serviceable candle, she came to the bed and looked down at him. "You look pale. The bleeding has stopped. Just lie still. Do...you...understand?"

Joel stared up at her and scowled. Seconds before, the pounding in his brain had offered to stop. If he could just hold Fiona close. She had spoken to him as if he was a half-wit. She was the only person, except his father, who had ever spoken to him in that tone. It nettled—Joel was accustomed to giving orders, not receiving them. He rubbed his aching temple. "Don't you ever get tired of giving orders?"

She quickly ran her hands down slender hips encased in jeans. "It's what I do best. There's a freshwater creek out back. I'll bring in water. Those cuts need cleaning, but your face looks like you've already had the experience."

He'd had plenty of experience, beginning with his father's hands. But now, tough Joel Palladin desperately needed to feel Fiona's hands on him. He damned himself for his weakness, his need of anyone, and swept out a hand, claiming her slender wrist. "You'll clean the cuts for me, won't you?"

A woman who called her own terms, she gauged him with a hard look. "You'll have to do what I say. It will hurt."

"Sometimes hurting heals." Joel watched Fiona's eyes darken, and the air quivered between them. He understood: she was a survivor, not sparing him softness, but prepared to do what she must.

"Some things never heal," she said quietly and left the house. *His father had murdered her parents.* The past leaped between them, and Joel suddenly felt very old, burdened by images, guilt and boyhood hunger that he'd placed in a mental cupboard.

He sighed and allowed himself to doze, plastic rustling beneath his head. He had the woman he sought; all he had to do was to keep her close until he could handle the past and her.

At four o'clock in the morning, Fiona propped her sock-covered feet on an old wooden chair. Exhausted, she leaned back. She folded her arms across her chest and studied the man dozing restlessly on the bed.

After cleaning the wounds thoroughly, she'd sewn two stitches in each deep cut—she was adept at first aid, and a stint as a field nurse at a Montana commune had told her that butterfly bandages wouldn't service the cuts. Though the man turned pale, he didn't complain, even as she secured a square of disposable diaper over his wounds. He'd simply placed both hands around her waist and held her gently as she worked over him; he held her as though he were feeling her bones, sensing, angling to see what made her tick....

He was not used to being touched or cared for: a wary man, with dark brown hair that waved around his harsh face, softening it and flowing onto a neck tense with muscles. The candlelight was not kind to his face. It was all angles and jutting cheekbones, lean cheeks and, beneath a dark stubble, a jaw that was set and square. His nose had been broken, perhaps more than once. Oddly, amid the raw masculine features, his mouth seemed almost gentle.

His eyes were green, brooding, hard as jade and dark with tired shadows. He watched her as if he knew something she did not. Awakening briefly, he always found her in the darkness, latching on to her with his eyes as if he would never let her go. He clearly had his secrets, but she had hers, and their eyes had locked and warred. Fiona had had to look away, wary of the heat and shadows she found in his eyes.

"Call me Joel," he'd said earlier, as she'd propped him in a chair while she covered the new mattress with bedding.

Since it was only fair, she'd given him her name, and he'd tried it on his lips, a soft purring sound, "Fiona." He'd said it again as though testing the curl of it around his tongue, as if she'd just given him a gift. A shiver had jarred Fiona, his tone intimate, masculine, longing.

When he had tried and failed to undress, Fiona had gently leaned him against a wall and had deftly undone his belt, unzipped his jeans and had eased him into bed.

"You've done this before," he had murmured, unsettling her by wrapping his hand around her wrist.

While she was a woman who rushed through life, devouring it and speeding on to her next challenge, he was a "toucher" she decided, a man whose pleasures ran to lingering over a woman's softer skin. His disturbing tone had insinuated she'd had legions of lovers.

"I told you. I have brothers," she'd said, not wanting to give him any portion of her life.

"I'm sorry for what happened to you. That it was so hard on you," he'd whispered, drifting into sleep.

He probably meant how she had dodged the thieves' bullets. Fiona inhaled. What had happened to her? Everything? Nothing. She'd lived, survived and flown through life, suiting herself, and she was tired, so tired of fighting.

Joel—with a snarling, fighting dragon tattooed on his upper arm—that was all she knew of him. There was more, an angular lean body, corded and hard, weighing more than she'd expected, packed with solid muscle. He admitted to nothing, leaving her to assumptions. She'd collected a secret-keeper and she needed him. Fiona resented the tall, lean muscular man tossing on the bed. Taking care of him had slowed her down and had added to her fatigue.

On the other hand, though he didn't know it, he had provided safety for Eunice. Everything came with a price, Fiona decided wearily...and she had paid her share of them.

Joel's eyes opened, gleaming in the firelight coming from the old stove. He stared at her, and time stretched into a full minute, and then he shivered, his eyes locked with hers, the shadows trembling, hovering between them.

"Are you cold?" she whispered, and wondered if he was really awake, or if fever was setting in from his wounds.

"Talk to me," he murmured and shivered again.

"You should be warm enough," she worried aloud and rose, padding to him in her socks. She untied the king-size sleeping bag she'd found in his car, opened it and placed it over the down quilt covering him. "I checked the car's registration in the glove box. The name was Pete Glass, not Joel."

"I haven't had time to—"

"Sure." Fiona slashed at him flatly, angry with herself that she had collected a car thief on her way to save Eunice. "Don't you think that a down feather bed is a strange thing for a man to carry around in the back of a tiny sports car? And this down comforter? They should both be warm enough."

They were new, a cash register tape had tumbled from their sacks. Joel Whoever shopped in pricey stores. Or whoever owned the sports car before it was stolen liked expensive, lush bedding—the down comforter was of a masculine brown and black design, the sheets and pillowcases striped in the same shades.

"Talk to me," he repeated.

She was too tired, and that was when she was most vulnerable. Impatient with her weakness, she spoke sharply, "Look, we both need rest. You most of all—"

He frowned slowly, studying her with those quiet green eyes, firelight gleaming on his dark skin, hard bones thrusting beneath the surface. "You're protecting yourself," he said. "Not wanting to give me anything. I know the feeling. Are you afraid of me? I won't hurt you."

He'd caught her unprepared for that quick, perfect insight, and she tensed. "Why should I be afraid of you? You're the one stretched out, wearing my stitches and helpless. I'm still on my feet and ready to walk out the door when it suits me."

Joel simply sighed and wearily closed his eyes. After his second shiver, Fiona shook her head. She was exhausted, too wound up to sleep, and feeling fragile, an emotion she rarely allowed herself. When Joel shivered again, Fiona sighed. He needed body heat. She sat on the bed next to him, watched him shiver again, and, shaking her head at the folly of lying next to a man who looked this tough and worn, she slowly eased beneath the sleeping bag. "I'm right here."

He found her hand, curling his larger, rougher one around it. She hadn't expected the calluses. Fiona stiffened, ready to withdraw her hand, then she surrendered to the oddly familiar comfort of a male's larger hand enfolding hers, a selfish need that she was too tired to deny. Slowly, so slowly, his head eased over to her pillow, sharing it, and she studied him as he slept. "You'll be lucky if your temperature stays down. You look exhausted and you're going to ache down to your bones tomorrow. It *is* tomorrow," she corrected.

Fiona stared at the firelight flickering on the old ceiling, which needed plastering. She'd come so many miles, fought so hard, and she found herself speaking. "Last December, I came home for Christmas."

She glanced at Joel, who appeared to be sleeping. The sound of her voice would comfort him; her words wouldn't matter. "There I was, just in from battling, saving another historical site from being blasted by developers and suddenly I was dead tired. I didn't have anything left. I wanted my family."

Fiona smiled softly, listening to the man's even breathing, and knew that he slept. He wouldn't remember her secrets, and she needed to talk, even to a stranger she'd collected at a convenience store holdup. "You're not so bad, Joel. You don't like being ordered, the blaze of your eyes and the way you tense your body tells me that. I've got brothers who act like that. I've always liked having the upper hand, though, and I'm used to getting my way."

He sighed heavily, his breath brushing her throat.

Fiona blinked away the tears that suddenly sprang to her lids. "I have a big family. There's my oldest brother Duncan, then Calum, Birk and my sister Elspeth. I'm the youngest and they've all worried about me all my life, especially when my parents were killed in a convenience store holdup. My folks had stopped by to pick up pizza for us. We were waiting at home, and they interrupted a robbery. My brothers tracked the killer into the mountains—they were the only trackers who could follow the trail at night up into the wilderness, and the sheriff knew it. They brought him back, but my parents were never coming back. They're buried up on Tallchief Mountain."

She leaned her head against Joel's, needing the touch of life.

"Suddenly, last Christmas, I knew I had to come back, to watch Megan, Daniel, Kira and Elspeth's Heather and all the rest of the babies that would come into the Tallchief family. Now there's Birk and Lacey's Willow and—I had to be here. I had to come back and settle what was in me somehow. I had to have peace. I'm too tired, Joel. I'm missing something inside me. Maybe I've given it away, piece by piece."

He continued to breathe evenly, deeply, and Fiona inhaled. "It helps to grow things and please people with my plants and flower arrangements—I own a florist shop with a small greenhouse. I'm tired of causes, Joel, and except for this time, I've been minding my own business. I'd like to find a man. Not that I believe in fantasy or love, but I have a biological clock ticking, you know, especially with all the babies my family is producing. I've got this awful, sinking feeling that I need a conventional relationship, a man to make me happy, a house to tend and reams of children to pass on the Tallchief legends. You could say that I'm lonely. Or that a piece of me is missing."

She tapped her fingers and settled more deeply into her thoughts. "Or perhaps I'm sexually hungry. I have this awful feeling that if the right man touches me, I'll change and never be the same. I feel as if…as if I'd tear off my clothes and have him on the spot. I'm a savage when I want something badly. It's darned hard being the last virgin, you know. No, you probably wouldn't know."

Joel issued a taut shudder and a groan. She yawned after he settled close to her side. "I'm a difficult woman. I've been told that often enough. But every one of the legends attached to Una's dowry has materialized. Una was my great-great-grandmother, a Scottish indentured servant who was captured by a Sioux chieftain, Tallchief. They fell in love, and to save Tallchief land, she sold her dowry. Just after my parents died, we each pledged to return a portion of it to our family. My family has done their share, and each legend attached to the dowry has come true."

She stretched, the warmth of bedding and the man beside her seducing her into sleep. Joel moved her hand onto his chest, and she allowed the trespass and the comfort. "I pledged to find Una's sewing chest. According to her journals, it's small, wooden and brass, but filled with sewing clutter—tatting shuttles, needles, thimbles and buttons. The odd things my grandmothers before Una treasured, tiny bits of their lives, like Celtic jewelry. The legend has to do with the oddest thing—a circle. Of course, the Celts fashioned intricate designs, based on everything relating, coming full circle, so it's no wonder. And my Native American heritage says everything is related, a part of everything else, forming a whole.''

Joel sighed heavily, almost abruptly, startling her. Fiona watched him for a moment and then decided that a bruise had hurt him as he moved.

She continued, freewheeling through her thoughts. ''I want lust. Good old-fashioned lust and desire for a man who makes me happy...and who I make happy. I want to be desired, Joel, really desired, so much that deep down in my bones I feel the heat vibrating, pouring off me. I want to laminate myself to him, breathe his breath, taste him, revel in what I am—a woman—and then I'll feel complete. I want our skins to simmer, our bones to lock, our mouths to taste and lick and devour. I want to really know him, taste him down one side and up the other. I want the sounds of our lovemaking to boil our brains. I want to feast on him and him on me, and I want an orgasm so deep and so perfect and so unique that I'll spin off into the moon, the stars. I want to wallow in afterplay—''

She paused as Joel's big body lurched unexpectedly and he groaned lightly, unevenly. She waited for him to settle again and continued, ''Though I've been prowling, trying to fit different men into an image of giving me the ultimate release, I've never lain on a bed with a man before—other than my brothers when they were comforting me as a child,'' she whispered as he continued to sleep. ''You're my first, Joel Whoever-You-Are, and though you're the size of a mountain, I'm not exactly helpless. So just sleep on and dream of another sports car to steal and let me talk. It's seldom that I stop long enough to let anyone know what is in my mind or my heart, and you should consider yourself one lucky guy. And for me, it's cheap therapy.''

Fiona closed her eyes and opened them to the fingers of fire-light playing in the shadows. ''I want no easy lover, but an even match. I want to feel his heart racing against mine and know that his desire for me is as true as Tallchief's was for Una—keep in mind that I'm not wanting love, that would be too much to ask. That when he gives himself to me, I'll know I have something he's never given another woman, and that the fire is only between us, hot enough to meld us into one, if only temporarily, and then..." She inhaled slowly. "I want to know what my great-great-grandmother and the rest and my sister and brothers have felt. But now I'm home where my roots are, and I just know that I'll find what I need in Amen Flats."

Fiona traced his chest with her thumb, his hand covering hers. "You'll forget all about this private conversation, won't you? So you won't mind if I tell you the legend, will you? It's so strange— *To finish the circle, an unlikely love of the battlemaiden will come calling, bearing his angry dragon on one arm and the chest to win her heart. Then the magic circle will be as true as their love.*"

She lay quietly for a moment, tangled in the warmth of the man sleeping beside her and the legend curling through her mind. "Una wrote other things, like how his kisses stopped her fiery mouth, and how the magic ran like heated sunlight and honey between them, and her with her stitching and him with his dreams came to make the circle complete...how he gentled her heart in the end. I think she gentled him, too—rather she tamed him. It's a lovely fairy tale. Love is a fairy tale for me, though I know my brothers and sister have found it. I have no illusions about love entering my life. I've tried it, and the shoe doesn't fit. It always causes pain, and I've had enough, seen enough, not to want more. I just want good, solid physical contact. I'm a physical woman who understands her body's needs. I like action, and I've never kissed a man yet who could make me want to—"

She yawned, sliding into the warmth of the bed and badly needed sleep.

He was here, the man she sought, the dream lover. He'd come before, just once, and when she'd awakened he was gone. She trusted him now, giving herself to his touch. She floated in the soothing warmth, the big warm hand lightly stroking her cheek, fitting itself to her, cupping. She sighed, moving her head slightly, turning to the irresistible safety, and a man's thumb ran lightly across her lips. She kissed it softly and turned her body to his, irritated with the heavy layers separating them.

Fiona wanted him close to her, so close that nothing separated them. She eased closer, arching against his length. Oh, yes, he fitted her perfectly, all hard and warm and so...so tender.

She lifted her face, giving him her mouth, and his light, tender kisses tasted of honeyed dreams and love and happiness. To draw him closer, Fiona slid her hands up to his throat, seeking his strong pulse, wanting him closer until they were one. His lips eased softly upon hers, and she tasted the dreams inside him, let them curl around her.

She splayed her fingers through his hair, letting it curl around them as she drew him nearer.

His hands were large and firm and yet so light, trembling as they touched her shoulders, her back, her waist...a man who knew what he wanted and who took it, though his ways enchanted and tantalized.

He groaned softly as if desiring her more than air, and his hands opened, claimed, fitting her hips to his.

She changed the kiss, slanted it, fused her lips to his, wanting the heat she knew he'd give, the desire she tasted on his tongue....

His breath swept across her, and she dived into the flavors of desire, dreams and shadows.

He moved as if to draw away, and Fiona slid over him, claiming him with her body, seeking his lips, touching his tongue with hers, suckling him to the rhythm of her desire.

She had been right...she was a woman of action, not waiting to take what she wanted. He was meant for her alone.

He tasted of her dreams, her love, the legend of the dragon-lover, the circle coming true—

Heat pounded through her, wrapped in desire. She hurled herself into the storms, the hunger and—

She blinked, trembling, the savage need humming through her as she looked down at the man she had captured.

He was still sleeping, his lips swollen with her kisses. Fiona trembled, forced herself to lie very still, shocked that his body wanted her—his hands were open, warm, firm and knowing. Beneath her jeans, one hand cupped her bottom, bringing her tight against his hardness. The other cradled her breast, a thumb brushing the tip, tantalizing her. Joel's dark cheeks were flushed, heat pouring off him, a pulse pounding in the vein at his temple—

"I want to be in you, a part of you.... Kiss me," he ordered arrogantly in his sleep, as if he had that right, as if he were her lord and master. The drawl was rich, sleepy, masculine and loaded with sensuality.

Fiona shivered. While Joel was still sleeping, she was fully awake and too aware of the danger of the moment. His hand moved up to the back of her hair, toyed with the short-chopped lengths and gently urged her head down to his. Fiona resisted, pushing back.

His lids opened slightly; he stared at her for a heartbeat, shook his head, as if to clear it. Then with a shudder and a disgusted groan, Joel sank back into sleep.

Fiona stared at him, temper simmering. *This bozo was dreaming of another woman, while he made love to Fiona!*

Incensed, Fiona held her temper. She couldn't hurt an injured, probably delirious, dreaming man; it wasn't honorable to pick on the defenseless. She lay upon him, aware that one big hand still claimed and caressed her bottom beneath her briefs. She slowly eased his hand out of her jeans and taking care, lifted her body from on top of his. Joel sighed deeply and reached out an arm, curling it around her waist. "Don't leave me, not yet," he whispered close to her ear and gently bit her lobe.

Fiona lay very still within the circle of his arm, the comforter between them. All she needed in her life now was that her first turn-on should be by a man who obviously knew how to make love in his sleep, a man who thought he held another woman in his arms. "Listen, you—" she began.

"Shut up. You talk too much. You're giving me a headache," he grumbled sleepily. He drew the sleeping bag over her, turned her as easily as a child and fitted his tall body to her back, spoon fashion.

She lay very still, and when twenty minutes had passed, Fiona decided that if she wasn't the woman he really wanted, she might as well take advantage of his comfortable warmth. In time she dozed again, aware of Joel sleeping deeply, holding her lightly.

* * *

Joel awoke at noon. Every inch of his body hurt, and the stitched wounds in his head throbbed. He eased a hand to his side, pressed the bruised flesh and decided his ribs were not broken.

For a heartbeat he wallowed in fantasy, dispatching himself from the shield he'd welded around his emotions. He inhaled Fiona's fresh wildflower scent, wallowed in it and prowled through the other scents to the one that reminded him of babies. Hell, yes, he admitted reluctantly. He wanted babies, he wanted a house filled with them. He wallowed in the image of Fiona's long, slender body filling with his child.

A man who dealt with cold reality, Joel placed the image in a mental drawer. He might desire Fiona Tallchief, his body needing relief, but fantasy and babies weren't for him. His ex-wife had said he was unromantic, cold and calculating. Patrice was probably right; he liked his life neat and uncomplicated. He gingerly touched the plastic square covering his cuts, remembering Fiona snipping the square and concentrating on securing the disposable diaper with duct tape.

Joel turned slowly, his head pounding, to the old table near the fire, piled with the foodstuffs from his car, his leather bag and Fiona's olive drab backpack. He'd dreamed that she'd stripped in the morning light, warmed by the stove that she had just stoked. He closed his eyes and the vision of long, feminine curved legs, backlit by the fire behind her, caused him to shudder.

Her towel, one of the big lush ones he'd just bought, was tossed over the back of a chair.

Joel groaned unevenly. His head wasn't alone in pain; his body was throbbing, jerking to life when he remembered how she had heated water in the metal bucket, and used a cloth to soap her face, rinsing, and then proceeding to the sheen of her bare shoulders above the towel. By the time she'd reached her long legs, bracing one on the chair, Joel's fists had been wrapped in the sheets and his body was painfully aware that it had been five years since he'd—

He frowned, the bruises on his forehead throbbing. He wanted more from Fiona than a fast sexual release.

Her tight, white sweater had clung to every taut curve, her jeans molded to slender hips and long legs. She'd whipped a black leather vest over the sweater and jammed on her boots. She'd stood, bracing her long legs apart as she'd slid beaded earrings into her ears and looped a chain over her head, looking nothing like the slender boy who had claimed Joel.

The light had flowed over her curves and words plowed through Joel's throbbing head—*ripe...feminine, sweet, savage, hot...and his,* though she didn't know it. Joel inhaled slowly, forcing himself to think. He hadn't intended to find Fiona so quickly, but now that he had, she wasn't—

"You'll be fine," she had whispered over him, smoothing his hair back from the diaper square. "There's canned soup when you're hungry. Just stoke up the stove and then you should sleep. I'll be back this afternoon. Rest," she'd said in the tone of a woman who expected her orders to be obeyed.

He'd never liked orders, nor the thought of a woman—or anyone—taking charge of him. Joel sat up slowly, ignored his bruises and the pounding in his head and swung his legs over the side of the bed. He was weaker than he thought and forced himself to walk to his bag, where he fished out a mobile telephone. He flipped it open, jerked up the antenna, punched in his brother's number and hoped the high-tech telephone wouldn't be stopped by a few sky-high Rocky Mountains.

After Rafe answered, Joel said, "I'm at the ranch. Fiona Tallchief has...nabbed me. See what you can find out about what she's been up to, will you?"

"Are you okay?" The Palladins always took care of each other, and Rafe's tone said that he'd be at Joel's side if needed.

"Just peachy," Joel answered grimly. Drop a detail in Rafe's lap and he'd run with it. He didn't want Rafe or any other woman-hunting male anywhere near Fiona. "How's Cody? Still mad at me for jerking him away from his street pals and installing him at Mamie's?"

"He's peeved, but Nick and I are keeping him busy, doing all those things we didn't get to do as kids. Reminds me of when she reined us in." In the background, Rafe was already punching computer keys, "Nabbed you? Was that what you said? Fiona

Tallchief? Don't tell me you've met your match, the great swash-buckling Joel Palladin.''

"There was a bit of trouble. And you know I tossed my swash-buckling into the bushes long ago," Joel said. Rafe knew Joel's weaknesses too well, and being saved by a woman hadn't helped his Iron Man image. "I was weak as a baby. She had me hauled out of there to safety like a bag of potatoes. Don't call me, I'll call you." Joel clicked the telephone off, killing the sound of Rafe's roaring laughter.

"He's mine...I'll take him," she'd said as though picking out a ripe tomato on a vender's cart. Then she'd proceeded to tell him about her needs as a virginal savage, a woman of action, which was enough to send him into a permanently hardened ache. She liked everything on her terms, purring along according to her directions.

The novelty of a woman claiming him, giving him orders caused him to frown. Fiona Tallchief had lessons to learn....

Three

Fiona nudged open the old door with her shoulder and carried in the two sacks of groceries. The daisy bouquet tucked under her chin hadn't suffered from being tied to her saddle horn. She lifted the small potted fern stuffed onto the top of the grocery sack and carried it to the old sewing room.

She placed it on the floor and studied the wonderful light she had shared with Mrs. Watkins. It was only five o'clock in the afternoon. She'd closed Hummingbirds early and hurried to her apartment above the shop. She'd had a quick, but luxurious shower, stuffed a change of clothes into her backpack, then hurried to the grocery store and on to Birk's to pick up Dante.

"You're all fired up and easy to read," her brother had said. "Since you came back in December, you've been busy setting up Hummingbirds, but something was missing and now it's back. You've got that sharp, hunting look. You're on a mission to save someone, something," Birk had stated flatly as he handed the reins of Joel's horse to her.

"It's handy to have brothers at times. In addition to keeping

Morning Star for me, you provide such good day care for other horses," she had tossed at him.

"I don't recognize this horse." Birk had stood, looking at her as if he knew every molecule of her plans. After years of experience with Duncan, Calum and Birk, she recognized that Black Knight look—one eyebrow raised, arms folded across his chest and long legs spread.

Because Birk had looked so worried, Fiona hurled herself at him, kissed his cheek and patted it. "His name is Dante. I love you. I'm safe, I'm well, and you can back off," she had ordered pleasantly.

The problem with overly protective brothers like the Black Knights was that they sometimes cramped her freedom.

Her forty-five-minute ride across the old mountain trail to the homestead had allowed her plenty of time to think. The objects of her crusades—Eunice and Joel—were in their designated places, and Danny's call informed her that all hell was breaking loose at the zoo. Fiona told him she wanted hell to simmer for a while, before exposing the intended sale of Eunice to the notorious Timba Simba Land, which had already been found guilty of exotic animal negligence. She didn't mention that Danny's rig had a few scratches caused by her bashing into a convenience store.

Despite her collecting Joel, things were perking along fine. Eunice was safe in the barn, pacified by Fiona's battery-operated radio. Though Joel's horse wasn't pleased at first with Eunice's snout investigating his body, he'd begun to accept the snout's actions as petting.

Lying on the bed, Joel looked as if he hadn't moved, his bare back turned to her and his shoulders tanned and gleaming above the expensive comforter. Fiona eased the sacks onto the table, pushed aside a clutter to make room and swung her heavy backpack down from her shoulder.

In that morning's dim light, his face had been swollen, the bruises starting to bloom into a glorious purple.

"You're a slob, Joel," she remarked pleasantly after glancing around the room. She stuffed the daisy, baby's breath and greenery bouquet into an old fruit jar and added water from the drink-

ing bucket. She surveyed the room slowly. He'd been up: his
T-shirt and shorts lay on the floor with a towel; a pan crusted
with hardened soup was proof that he'd eaten; and he'd tossed
the diaper square used as a bandage onto the floor. He'd rummaged through his overnight bag, and an array of silk boxer shorts
overflowed onto the table. The opened bottle of aspirin had been
used often, some of the tablets spilled on the table. He'd left the
dipper from the bucket of drinking water on the chair beside his
bed. Fiona capped the aspirin, jammed his clothing back into his
bag. She quickly changed into sweat clothes and hurried out to
forage in the old woodpile. In fifteen minutes she had carried in
a supply for the night, stoked up the old wooden cookstove and
filled its water reservoir with water from the nearby spring.

The old kerosene lantern, which she'd found in the same place
it had always been, and a few candles lit the old room, warming
it with memories. She placed the pot from her kitchen on the old
stove, took out the plates and cups and utensils resting in it. She
added chicken and water to the pot, dehydrated onions, garlic and
parsley, covering the broth as it simmered.

She almost enjoyed cleaning, she thought, as she dashed the
cobwebs away in the living room. The old homestead would be
the perfect place to keep Eunice while Danny drew the media's
attention to Timba Simba Land's intended purchase of Eunice.
Then the zoo would be under pressure, and a soft-hearted,
three-hundred-pound television reporter by the name of Brick
would make a perfect contact. She mopped around Joel's bed and
under it, bumping the legs as she worked. Brick's beautiful prose
concerning animal neglect could wring tears from—

"Will you stop that noise?" Joel demanded roughly, flipping
over to glare at her with the one eye that was not swollen shut.

"Hello, honey. I'm home from work. Enjoy your day?" Fiona
drizzled her tones in syrup. She was sweating from working,
while he slept in his cozy bed.

He scowled at her. "You've got a mouth," he said finally, and
turned away from her.

Fiona blew him a kiss, curtsied and, because she was riding on
a high of everything going her way, another crusade purring

along, she purposely bumped the bed again. Joel grunted and went back to sleep.

Fiona began to sing softly, pleased with herself, as she swept and mopped and stirred the chicken broth simmering on the stove, adding a sack of her neighbor's frozen homemade noodles.

She began a sultry Peggy Lee song, "Fever," and she added appropriate bumps and grinds as she mopped. Though the doors to the rest of the house remained closed, Fiona had to clean Mrs. Watkins' old sewing room, lined with windows and memories.

Broom in hand, and studying the fern in the moonlight, Fiona leaned back against the old wallpaper and sang the song Mrs. Watkins liked best, "Greensleeves."

Fiona gave herself to the memories, the past flowing back to her, wrapping around her. Through the tears in her eyes, she saw the man watching her from the other room. Shadows circled him, the lamp and candlelight touched his hard face, gleaming on the dark skin covering his cheekbones and flickering in his eyes, holding her in place like a doe caught in the sights of a hunter's rifle. The look held and frightened her, because the impact jarred her, reached inside her and foraged.

She hated him instantly. No one dared reach inside Fiona, except her family, and even they dared not pry too deeply, wary of wounding her.

Joel had seen too much; he'd seen her pain and loneliness, disguised from other people. Fiona dashed the tears from her eyes; she needed to escape Joel's intense, burning stare. "I'm going out to check on your horse and bring in more wood. It will be cold tonight. There is soup on the stove, if you want it."

"I'm sorry," he spoke softly again, confusing her. His tone had the impact of a bulldozer, stopping her in midstep.

Why? she asked mentally, then shoved the thought away. She faced him, squaring off, lifting her defenses. "Look, Joel. I've got no time for you, or your prodding, or your sympathies, whatever they are. You're someone I don't want to know. I'm temporarily storing my rig in your barn, and that's it. I just don't care about you."

He was quiet for a moment, then sighed wearily. "I care what happens to you."

Fiona ended the conversation by kicking the door that separated the sewing room from the living room. Satisfied with the loud slam that was certain to jostle Joel's headache, she moved through the cold shadowy house to the back door, forced it open and tromped to the barn. Eunice, always a good listener, promptly wrapped her trunk around Fiona, who leaned on the elephant and hugged her as she cried.

"Thank you, Eunice. I appreciate the hug," Fiona stated shakily. "I'm just tired, but don't you worry. Danny is stirring up the media right now, and with Brick on your side, everything will be fine. The man in the house cares about me only because right now I'm taking care of him...keeping him warm, fed and all the other comforts he needs. That's all it is."

After feeding Eunice and letting the gelding into the small field to graze, Fiona squared her shoulders. She'd never avoided a confrontation if one was necessary, and if Joel attempted any more—

A half hour later she kicked the front door closed with her boot and deposited the firewood in the old watering tub on the floor. Joel hadn't moved, the dim light angling over the breadth of his shoulders and the triangle of dark hair on his chest. Fiona poured the soup into a mug, stirred it with a spoon and walked to him. His eyes flickered open, and a jolt of awareness skittered up her spine. "You're pale. Have you eaten?" she asked.

His eyes slowly closed as if blocking her out. "I'm not hungry. Go away."

After living with her brothers, she knew how to handle contrary males. "You should eat. I'll help you."

More to taunt Joel than to feed him, Fiona sat down on the bed, placing the mug on the chair. "Sit up. You're going to eat now."

He lifted one lid, eyeing her. She went for the challenge like a cat after a mouse, immediately bending over him to draw the pillow up higher. He lay still, his neck oddly crooked, looking up at her.

"Up. If you don't eat, you'll never recover and then I'll never get rid of you," she ordered, pleased that his expression had changed to a dark scowl. "You know, if you keep lying there with your neck at an angle, it will be very stiff."

"Will you leave me alone if I eat?" he asked in a low, ominous drawl after a full moment.

"I may or I may not. I make no promises. I'm used to getting my way, Joel. You'd have an easier time of it, if you gave up now."

"Is that right?" he tossed back, the angle of his jaw hardening defiantly. "You like people under your thumb, surrendering to you, do you?"

"Uh-huh, that's about the size of it."

When Joel moved, she noted size—his. He looked as fit as any of her brothers, the dim light skimming across the width of his shoulders.

His bare chest shouldn't have unnerved her, caused her to look away as another jolt of awareness hit her.

"You look like hell. Hard day at the office, honey?" he tossed at her as he eased himself higher then rested back on the pillow. The dragon flexed over the muscle on his arm, and Fiona realized suddenly that she was staring at it, fascinated by the play of skin over muscle and—something darkened in Joel's eyes, heated the air between them. "Getting to you, am I?" he asked with a knowing, sensual curve to his beautiful mouth.

Fiona had little time for sensual games, and she wasn't playing them with a car thief. "Not likely. I could have you for breakfast and—"

"Mmm," he murmured slowly around the spoon in his mouth. His eyes darkened as if anticipating the thought that they would—

Fiona fought to keep her hand from trembling and quickly finished feeding him, too aware of the bedding lying low on Joel's flat muscled stomach. He was definitely aroused.

"Your hand is trembling. Don't be afraid. You don't need to be anymore," he said softly when she had finished.

"I am never afraid," she shot back and glanced down at his hand, which had come to rest on her thigh so lightly that she hadn't noticed. She eased it from her, wary of any contact with Joel.

"Aren't you?" he taunted her.

"I'm not in the market," she said flatly, aware that the conversation had taken a curve, undercurrents running through the air between them. She stood to her feet, eyes locked with Joel's green ones.

"Thanks for bringing me flowers. I've never had a woman bring me a bouquet before. You've done a nice job cleaning up the place.... When you're steaming, your eyes are the color of smoke. Why don't you tell me what really bothers you about me?"

Fiona straightened. Whoever Joel was, he knew just how and where to place his verbal jabs. She refused to answer, glaring at him until finally with an arrogant, pleased smile he turned his back to her and yawned. She, who had saved him, patched him, nursed him, cooked for him and cleaned, had been dismissed. Few people dismissed Fiona Tallchief, but she decided Joel wasn't up to a toe-to-toe discussion.

Oh, yes, he was. She rounded the bed so that he faced her. "Joel. Listen up. I'll help you start a new life. I'm good at that, reforming people, getting them set up. You need a nine-to-five job, with insurance benefits, and a decent neighborhood...a tidy little apartment that you can afford and that you can call home. You'll have to give up your old friends, of course. Because they'll draw you back down into crime. You've got to return that flashy car. I'll help you."

He opened one eyelid and winced. "I'd like to listen to your offer to make an honest man of me, really I would. But right now I've got a few aches and pains. A steak might help my eye, making the swelling go down."

Fiona tromped outside. She took a package from the apple box nailed to the outside of the house; in the cold temperatures, the box served as a refrigerator. Inside, she ripped open the paper, cut a piece off the huge steak and slapped it on his face. "There. Now will you listen to me?"

He eased the red meat from his nose to cover his blackened eye. "If I have to."

She sat on the bed, bounced on it hard, to get his attention. "You have to."

"Why don't you come to bed, and we'll talk about it?" The masculine drawl was meant to taunt her.

Fiona stared at him. Joel's invitation had set her senses tingling, disturbing her. She pushed away her uneasy emotions and pushed on with her cause, just as she had always done. "I'm trying to reform you. You could listen, or at least invest energy in bettering yourself."

"Talk," he said with a yawn, and lay back, steak over his eye, arms folded in front of his bare chest.

"You're too sleepy for it to have an effect." *She* was too sleepy to be effective.

"Fine," he murmured with another yawn. "I do need my sleep. I've had a hard week."

Fiona stiffened, impatient with the man she was trying to reform. "You've had a hard week. Isn't that too bad. I suppose thieving takes time and energy."

"There was that mountain of cans at the store," he added in a drawl, reminding her that she owed him. "I'll treasure the bouquet you brought me. Tomorrow, when you come home from work, could you bring some magazines? I like ones about cars."

"I just bet you do." Fiona whipped the sleeping bag from the bed and quickly zipped it up, flipped it on the floor and jerked a pillow from beneath his head. She held it for a moment wavering between bashing him and letting the matter drop.

"This mattress is great," he murmured sleepily. "Nice and soft, not too soft, but just right."

"You are not Goldilocks in the three bears' house. We'll talk later," Fiona said and dropped the pillow over his face.

At one o'clock in the morning, after taking away Joel's steak, checking on Eunice and trying to sleep fully dressed on the floor, Fiona surrendered to the temptation of one of Joel's soft T-shirts and a pair of his comfortable silk boxer shorts. Her car thief wallowed on a soft, warm bed, while she was left to the sleeping bag and a hard floor. The cab in the truck had a certain Eunice odor that Fiona could not abide.

Joel was sleeping deeply, and she was still wide awake, thrilled with the progress of exposing Timba Simba Land's proposed purchase of Eunice. While her mind streamed along at a hundred miles an hour, her body ached from exhaustion. She had to be at Hummingbirds in the morning, opening the shop as usual, or she could look suspicious. She got up, went to the bed and stared down at Joel. He looked safe enough, rather like her brothers, like someone she could trust. She eased on top of the comforter and drew the opened sleeping bag over her.

The old house creaked around her, the fire in the stove crackled, and Fiona sighed, wishing for sleep. She turned on her side away from Joel and back again. After fifteen minutes she decided to relieve her thoughts to the sleeping man, who wouldn't remember anything. "Joel, old buddy. You're not that bad, when you're asleep. You're the best therapy I've had in years."

He began to snore lightly, the sound pleasant, reassuring her that he was asleep and did not hear her.

Fiona lay perfectly still, listening to the October wind and circling on her emotions. October, the month of their parents' deaths, had always unsettled the Tallchiefs and raised their emotions—perhaps that was what she was feeling. The rhythm of Joel's light snoring provided a sense of safety.

He made her feel safe. There was no reason behind that emotion, just the sense that if she needed him, he'd be there. Like her brothers and sister, Fiona thought, snuggling down beside his warmth. "I used to sleep with my cats, and you're serving the same purpose, Joel. Poor Minnie, my cat at the shop. She's probably lonesome right now. Of course, she has Abe and George, my lizards."

Fiona listened to a branch rattle against a window. "I meant it when I said love wasn't for me. But I saw it in Mom and Dad and in my brothers' and sister's lives. I won't have anyone feeling sorry for me, Joel. I did what I had to do, growing up, and I was very good. Once the family wasn't in jeopardy, I took off like a shot, and yet, a part of my heart will always be here...so I came back. Last Christmas, I knew. I had to stop running and settle down. The florist business was up for sale, and I've always loved growing things. I've been bored, Joel. Really bored, and the men I've dated seemed scared of me. I've terrified the men in Amen Flats for years, and they know I'm not sweet. The rest...the other men I've dated just seemed so...drab."

He moved, shifting restlessly, and nudged his face against her cheek. Because he was still snoring lightly, she allowed the trespass and the pleasant weight of his arm sliding over her waist.

Fiona tapped her fingers on his arm, circling her thoughts. "I'll get you back on the right track if it kills me. Eunice and I appreciate your help."

She listened to the branch, scraping at the window. "I've been running too fast, Joel, and it has to stop. I feel as if I've given a piece of me away to each cause, and now there's nothing left for me. I love growing plants and I'd like a real garden someday, but just getting Hummingbirds up and running and remodeling my upstairs apartment has been hard. I'm making my stand, Joel. Our family challenge is to stand and fight, and that's what I'm doing. I'll know what I want when I see it."

She rubbed the tears from her eyes. "I'll lose myself, if I don't stop fighting, running here and there. I want a home, Mom's things where I can see them and frames to put my family's pictures in—not just the traveling wallet-size version in my tiny apartment over the shop. If home is where the heart is, Joel, then I've got to find it, because..."

She inhaled sharply, fighting tears. "I'm scared, Joel. Really, really scared. That missing part of me wants something that I don't know I can provide. My family is worried about me, and I hate that. Eunice understands. I tell her everything, even my need to experience a real laminating, heart-thundering, blood-boiling sexual experience. I know I'd want equality, that I'd want my share, because I've always been an active participant, and frankly I'm a bit greedy when it comes to filling my own more personal needs. Battling issues takes one part of me, but I am a physical woman, and a strong one. Sometimes the heat just pounds at me— you have no idea, Joel, because you probably take care of your sexual needs whenever you want, but I'm very, very picky, and a weak man won't do. I'd probably kill him. Or scare him. So many men want this passive, yes-whatever-you-want kind of woman, which I'm not."

On the pillow beside her, Joel groaned unevenly, and his body tensed. Fiona glanced at him scornfully. "Sure. Right. You're dreaming about it now, aren't you? That's because you know the moves and the heat and the final—whatever for men. Do you know that no man has even..."

She cleared her throat, uneasy with forming the words, yet determined to continue her therapy with Joel. "My breasts are untouched, Joel. They ache to be touched and yes, tended very well, by an experienced lover. That's all I want, an experienced well-matched lover. Make that a strong, physically fit, exciting lover. No commitment on either side. We both just take what we want, walk off and call it quits when the going gets rough...because I cannot handle any more emotional pain. I've just seen too much, and not only from when my folks were killed, but in the years I've been involved in environmental, human and animal rights."

Joel's arm shifted slightly, resting over Fiona's breasts. She closed her lids, her body aching in response to the pleasant weight. "Oh, fine. Just what I needed." She looked down at the dragon on his arm. His muscle flexed and it seemed to snarl at her. "You're asleep, or I wouldn't be telling you this. I've never told anyone, except Eunice, and she understands."

Joel reeled back as the bright October sunlight stabbed his eyes. He braced one hand against the post supporting the old porch, and it promptly cracked, threatening to break. He began walking toward the barn, easing his body back to life. The woman sharing his bed for the past two nights was tough, experienced at making do and probably could camp in the Rocky Mountains surrounding the ranch with ease. She caused him to feel delicate. Fiona moved quickly, competently and knew the basics of bathing with a bucket. She probably did terrify most men, especially when she started talking about sex and how Eunice understood.

Fiona Tallchief had all the symptoms of mental problems, with that imaginary friend she'd been talking to in the truck. Joel could deal with Fiona creating someone to be her friend; therapy could rid her of the need for a Eunice. But the way that low, sultry voice sang and beckoned to him, and Fiona's expression of her needs last night in bed, had caused Joel to awake like a teenage boy—

An independent and competent woman, she could stitch

wounds, make do with diapers instead of bandages and knew how to handle a big truck and trailer up and down steep grades and curves. *She'd brought flowers,* stuffing them into an old fruit jar and making the barren, cold house seem like home.

The sight of her this morning, padding to the old cookstove in his oversize T-shirt and shorts and her socks was almost endearing. He wasn't a man who treasured "endearing," except with Cody.

He missed so much of Cody's life, thanks to Joel's ex-wife. The blame wasn't hers alone, it was his for not pushing—Joel wondered if he was too late, if he could give Cody what he needed. Joel glanced at the field lying dormant near the barn. He was city-bred, just like his son, and they would learn together.

He glanced at the corral's broken fence and the old garden spot. He'd bought the ranch because of his specific needs for Cody, to have something to rebuild, to grow crops and animals and to build a relationship with his son.

He turned, shading his eyes against the dappled sunlight, and looked at the old house. It was a start. It needed plumbing and basic carpentry, and after he got his tools from the car, he'd check the old motor on the well's pump.

He retrieved the cellular phone tucked in his belt, and dialed Rafe's private number. His grandmother, Mamie Palladin answered. "Rafe is flirting with my secretary and getting nowhere. The girl has more sense than to let one of you Palladin boys interest her. You boys will have to stop ringing when I'm on my treadmill. I can't hear what's going on. Rafe is wearing his got-to-protect-my-brother look and you're the only one who I don't know what you're doing. I can't hear the conversation as well when I'm puffing away, and I know you're up to something, Joel, other than trying to rebuild your relationship with Cody. You don't need Rafe's help to get that old place up and running before winter...this project has 'leave me alone' Joel Palladin's signature all over it. So you're up to something. What is it?"

Joel smiled, loving his grandmother. Her interference had saved his life and his brothers'. "I try to keep you on your toes, Mamie. Otherwise you'd get bored."

"Don't you sweet talk me, Joel Palladin. I'll find out sooner or later. I always do. I love you," Mamie finished crisply.

Rafe picked up the line, and Joel tucked the mobile phone under his chin as he reached the barn. He lifted the board securing the barn's double doors. "What's Fiona Tallchief up to now?"

"She's stolen an elephant and tucked it away somewhere," Rafe stated just as Joel swung open the doors. He stepped into the darkness and ran into the hind end of an elephant.

"Is that right?" Joel asked softly after a moment, his eyes adjusting to the shadows. "I think I found it."

"Her name is Eunice. Timba Simba Land—TS Land—has been reported for animal neglect, and the zoo has approved the sale of the elephant to them. According to the zoo's spokesperson, Fiona Tallchief is a dynamic, forceful woman opposed to the sale. She tried allure, reason, and when she found that the zoo considered Eunice to be a piece of collateral and saleable property, she ignited. She's the suspect in the—" Rafe began to laugh "—elephant kidnapping. Apparently she's good at collecting things. She's got you, doesn't she? Collected you like a sack of potatoes, or something to that effect?"

"Stand by. I'll call you back." Joel hurriedly closed the doors and secured them from inside. He was small enough, in comparison to the elephant, to dive out the side door if she proved dangerous.

Joel was fascinated. As a child he'd never been able to get close enough to an elephant, and as an adult he'd forgotten or buried the wish. The elephant, not the largest he'd ever seen, was female, with an inquisitive trunk. Joel eased his lower body against his car and noted the peanut shells on the floor, fresh dung shoveled into a heap at one side, fresh hay and a washtub filled with water. To complete the cozy scene, a battery-operated tape deck played Elvis tunes, and a jar filled with daisies stood on a windowsill. Joel spoke quietly, not wanting to frighten the elephant, who seemed to wear a friendly smile, her tiny eyes flirting with him. He glanced at a huge ball and a child's red wagon. The elephant shoved the wagon at him gently with her trunk, then she indicated the gunnysack in the rafters above his head.

Joel obeyed, climbing up the old ladder to dig into the sack and toss peanuts down into her red wagon. "Eunice" was scrolled on the ball and the wagon. "Eunice," Joel murmured slowly. "Eunice, old girl. I thought you were a figment of Fiona's mind. I don't think anyone would call you a figment."

After he descended the ladder and began to feed her, Eunice wrapped her trunk around him and swayed, enclosing him in an elephant hug. Uncomfortable and wary, Joel allowed his body to be fondled intimately as Eunice prowled for more peanuts. "So our friend, Fiona Tallchief, has some explaining to do, hasn't she?" he asked Eunice.

The elephant's trunk wrapped around him provided little soothing to Joel's rising temper. He was a respected attorney, *and* an accomplice to grand theft. He allowed Eunice to hug him and sway as he called Rafe. "That elephant will be back in the zoo's keeping by Thursday morning. Keep the press out of it."

Rafe laughed. "Can't. There's a television bleeding heart named Brick who has exposed the somewhat-shady sale. Now tell me why you're interested in protecting the lady. Or do you like wearing sludge?"

Joel disconnected the line and whipped off the tarp covering his Corvette. "Sorry, Eunice. I've got to make a little trip into Amen Flats to visit your friendly florist and kidnapper. I'll be damned if I'll be listed as an accomplice in the zoo's break and enter and the transport of stolen goods across state lines."

He backed the car out of the barn, closed the doors and stopped. Joel leaned back against the car and studied the mountains, the morning sunlight on the old house. *Fiona Tallchief, all volatile, five-foot-ten, contrary, fascinating, sexy inches of her, was his and he was staking his claim.*

He would taste her, enjoy her and walk away, closing that ragged, disturbing edge that had bothered him since she'd dumped sludge over his designer suit.

After chewing on the fact that she aroused him like no other woman had in his lifetime, Joel called Rafe. "Get Nick in on this."

"Anything you want. This sounds serious."

"As serious as it gets." Joel checked his watch. "I want something dropped off at the ranch. Just bundle it up and have Nick parachute it down to me. It's old, fragile and precious, so wrap it carefully. It's eight o'clock now. I'll wait until eleven o'clock keeping Eunice company and getting to know her. That gives you three hours to get what I want and deliver it. This is what I want—"

He briefed Rafe, Palladin, Inc.'s project development affairs officer. Nick, a troubleshooter for Palladin, Inc., was the baby of the Palladin brothers. Nick could waltz a low-flying private jet through treacherous mountain canyons. The three brothers shared a bitter past, the ability to make any motor purr, an addiction to details, the love of their grandmother and a great big callus where man-woman love was concerned.

"Keep me posted," Joel finished, and settled back in the sunlight with his thoughts. United, the three brothers were tough, determined and capable of accomplishing anything. Once Joel delivered what Fiona wanted, the game would be on.

Joel found himself smiling. He swung open the door to the barn, patted Eunice's broad hind end and circled her. He stopped and studied her, noting her little eyes were warm and friendly. He stepped up on the truck, jerked open the cab door and pulled out the *Simple Everyday Elephant Care* handbook. Flipping through it, he braced himself for Eunice's inquiring trunk. After a moment he eased Eunice's trunk away from his lap and said, "Come on. You need some sunlight and exercise. You shouldn't be any trouble to get back into the barn. According to this and Fiona's notes on you, you'll go anywhere for peanuts and a good Elvis Presley song."

Four

Over the top of a bouquet of lush red roses Mr. Higgins had ordered for his wife, Fiona studied her brothers. On their mid-morning coffee break, Duncan wasn't really interested in her ferns, even though he loved growing them; and Calum was an unlikely fan of calla lilies. Birk, the father of his two-month-old daughter, Willow, was prowling through a new shipment of baby's breath as if it fascinated him.

Fiona took her time arranging, snipping and dressing the bouquet, letting her tall, brooding brothers prowl around her tiny shop cluttered with a rainbow of flowers, greeting balloons, and bows. Periodically, as if checking the doors to the fort, they glanced at the door leading to her upstairs apartment and to the narrow, cluttered hallway leading back to her tiny, but efficient green-house.

"Okay. You've come. You've looked and you're wondering," she stated with a smile. She loved them without reserve, and that love spilled over onto the women they had married and their families.

Duncan, Calum and Birk lined up against a counter and folded their arms across their respective broad chests. Duncan, the eldest, wore his ranch clothes, a rugged Westerner down to his boots. His mouth, grimly set, was softened by a smudge of Sybil's new russet lipstick. A former meticulously groomed businessman, Calum wore a sweater his wife, Talia, had knitted him, one sleeve too long and turned back and another too short. The white spots on his jeans indicated bleach and his usually neat hair was rumpled, his lips slightly swollen. Talia delighted in leaping into his well managed, organized world and kissing him until he steamed.

Birk, dressed in his construction clothes and work boots, had a pink baby rattle tucked into his shirt pocket. Peeking over the top of his other pocket was a bit of feminine lace and a tiny bra strap; he'd just come from taking Willow down to see her mother, Lacey, at the construction site. Lacey and Birk shared and alternated parenting and Tallchief Construction duties.

Fiona adored them, each deeply in love and still finding time to worry about her. She grinned at them. "I know you didn't just drop in to check out my fresh-cut flowers. I don't need furniture moved in my upstairs apartment or my water spraying system checked."

Fiona glanced at her front display window and smiled as Elspeth swept into the shop. Tucked closely against Elspeth was three-month-old Heather Petrovna, with a cap of wild black curls. "I was just in town seeing to a shipment. The gallery in Denver is doing a marvelous job displaying my new merino shawls."

The big, tough Tallchief brothers melted into warm jelly, gathering around Heather, who blinked up at them with big gray eyes. Duncan hugged Heather against him. "Daniel has over six months on you, but you'll be catching him soon," he crooned, kissing the tiny fingers that had wrapped around his finger. "Megan can't wait for you to play dolls with her. I'll come to your tea parties just like I did with Mommy and Aunty Fiona, and so will Daniel."

Sunlight slid in a shaft through the shop's window, touching the Black Knights and Elspeth, each with glistening black hair and smoky gray eyes to match Fiona's. They were the best part of her, settling the emptiness in her heart, if only for the moment.

"Okay, I've been up to something this past weekend," she

admitted, feeling guilty because they had always worried about her. "But I can handle it, it's something I want to do, and I'm really, really good at doing this."

"She's always had that defiant look when she knows we'll disapprove of whatever she's got bubbling on her back burner," Calum noted clinically.

Fiona smiled brightly at them, stepping into the game dappled with love and teasing. "You know I only cook enough to survive. I've been living off real food at your tables since December."

Elspeth looked at her brothers' dark, intent expressions and said, "You're not getting it out of her. She's got that look. See the angle of her chin and the fire in her eyes? On the other hand, maybe Fiona would like to come to my house for dinner tonight and I'll cook your favorite spaghetti. Alek will be gone, working late at the paper and you can help me with Heather."

Fiona grinned. "Can't. I'm busy. Intrigue, you know. The bubbling pot and all that. You can't get it out of me, either, Elspeth. Not for sweet little dumpling Heather, or tasty pasta and fresh baked bread. So Alek won't have to leave his nice warm house tonight, just so you can pry my dark secret from me, torturing me with second helpings and old movies that make me cry."

Elspeth sighed. "It used to work on you."

Duncan scowled. "You've been moping around here for months, looking like nothing could bring out that wicked, impish grin from you again, and—"

"Suddenly, you're revved up and blooming," Calum finished. "You've got that—"

"Look," Birk supplied. "Fiona the fiery is back in business."

Fiona placed a rosebud over one ear of each of her siblings. "One last run," she said. "Then I'll settle down. This really has to be done. Oh...no..." she finished as a low-slung Corvette squealed to a stop in front of Hummingbirds.

Joel erupted from the small car with all the force of a volcano, leaping onto the sidewalk with a small, paper-wrapped object under one arm. He was dressed as she had first seen him, in his worn jacket, jeans and boots. He scowled down the length of Amen Flats' Main Street and then strode through Hummingbirds' front door.

The little bell overhead tinkled merrily in direct contrast to Joel's dark scowl. He surveyed the Tallchief family coolly. "Let's skip the introductions. You're Duncan, you're Calum, you're Birk and you're Elspeth. All Tallchiefs."

Fiona's heart stopped as Joel leveled a dark, deadly glare at her. He'd shaved, his rugged jaw clenched tight and unyielding. The distinctive cleft in the center of his chin reminded her of someone...dressed in an expensive suit. Someone who, drenched in the sludge she'd just poured over him, looked as though he could pack her over his shoulder. "You are Joel Palladin. Joel! I should have— Get out of my shop, you—"

"I am not—repeat—not a predator of the environment." He placed the small, wrapped package on her counter, amid the roses she had been arranging.

"Palladin?" Duncan asked slowly, as if testing the name.

Joel turned to look at Duncan. "That Palladin," he repeated firmly.

A look that Fiona did not understand passed between her brothers and sister and Joel. One by one, he met each of their questioning looks and then turned back to Fiona.

She had no time to deal with whatever ran between Joel and her family; she had no time to waste in tearing Joel apart.

"This could get messy," Fiona said firmly, standing on tiptoe to look over Joel's shoulder at her family. "You might want to leave."

"Not a chance," they returned just as grimly.

"Open it," Joel ordered, his deep raw tone slicing into the air.

"No," she shot back, furious with him.

"Fine. I will." Joel's big hand whipped away the paper to reveal a small wooden chest, decorated with Celtic brass buttons. He shot the words at her like bullets, repeating Una's legend, "To complete the circle, an unlikely love of the battlemaiden will come calling, bearing his angry dragon on one arm—"

Joel ripped off his worn leather jacket and tossed it to the counter, revealing the dragon tattoo on his arm. He continued to quote as he drew on his jacket, the collar up, "The angry dragon on one arm and the sewing chest to win her heart. Fantasies and legends...darn...you just can't beat 'em."

Fiona shook, rage blooming in her. *"You weren't sleeping when I told you that!"*

Joel's eyes flashed, emerald bright, between his narrowed lashes. "Darling, I was fascinated by every word."

"Sleeping? You slept with him? That doesn't sound like you," Duncan asked sharply.

Fiona slashed out her hand, silencing her oldest brother and turned to Joel. "You—you listened to everything, you jerk. Don't be so shocked, Duncan. I've slept with men before, fully dressed and in my own bedroll. It's not what you think. I had to rescue him—"

She straightened, shocked and outraged by how much she had done for Joel Palladin. "I actually cooked and cleaned for you. You rich, spoiled, self-indulgent, environment-wrecking, arrogant, macho—"

"She cooked and cleaned *and* slept with me. She's determined to save me and find me a decent job," Joel underlined Fiona's words, fueling her temper. She wanted to hurl the new shipment of clay pots at him, one by one.

He smiled coldly and leaned back against the counter. He lifted the chest's lid idly and let it snap shut. "I haven't looked inside, Fiona the fiery. You'll be the first to see inside since the elderly lady, who owned it, polished the brass interior. It's fascinating, isn't it? That something...someone would wait for years for just the right person?"

He turned to the other Tallchiefs. "We're past the first courting stage—flew by it when she introduced that truck to the store. I had plans to present myself like a gentleman and try a customary date or two. You see, I had some grand notion that she might tell me she's sorry for dumping sludge over my head, if I introduced myself properly and explained my position on the environment. But, oh, no. Fiona tossed all that away, plowed through it with all the tenderness of a bulldozer. There's only one way to handle a woman like her. Jump into the storm and hold on. I think I can do that and give her what she wants. I've got the dragon and the chest. She's temporarily mine it would seem, according to Una's legend, and I intend to claim what is mine."

For a moment the Tallchiefs were quiet, and Joel surveyed

them with the look of a gunfighter ready for a showdown. Fiona wanted to wrap her hands around his muscled throat and—

"I knew she looked guilty each time that truck, smashing into the convenience store, was brought up. You see, Joel, our parents were killed in that same sort of store holdup. But your handling of Fiona is not exactly—" Elspeth began.

The Tallchief brothers looked dark, brooding and about to call Joel out onto the street. Fiona had to defend him; her brothers were tough country boys—on the other hand, Joel's taut, grim look said he'd stepped into an alley or two in his time.

"The oversaturation of old-fashioned males in this room is bad for my plants' vibes. Palladin is all mine. Don't you dare interfere. I can handle him," Fiona stated very quietly, meaning it. "He's out of his league."

After a long, tense moment, Birk asked, "What was in the eighteen-wheeler, Fiona the fiery?"

She silenced Joel with a frown. "Keep out of this. Don't say a word."

He shrugged, looking bored and innocent, and she could have dumped the plant food she'd been mixing on him.

"She's at her best when she's all fired up, and I seem to have the ability to do that. I think she's the most fascinating, beautiful—not in a classic way—but an enchanting, feminine blend just the same. Rather like a long, tall, very independent and capable, exotic elf."

He flipped open the chest, plucked out a small ring made of horsehair and blue beads and slipped it on her finger. "Sorry, you can't have everything exactly your way, Princess. You've gone too far. You're mine, you see, and you know it," he added as he placed an intricate tiara made of brass, twisted into a Celtic design, on her head.

Fiona discovered her mouth was open. She closed it and locked her eyes with Joel's dark green ones. They were darker than ferns, more the shade of a meadow at sundown...or was it— She felt herself go light-headed and gripped the counter for support.

His fingers winnowed through her short hair for a moment; when she slashed his hand away, he caught her wrist and leveled a look at her family. "We'll be gone for a couple of days. We're returning the elephant she stole in Missouri. I am an attorney, and it appears that I am also her accomplice. I really do not like my career and reputation threatened by a pachyderm thief. I'm certain you don't want your baby sister brought up on interstate trafficking, grand theft and any other little thing she's done, including ramming that convenience store.''

He faced the Tallchiefs who were studying Fiona closely. "I'd rather not fight you, but I would. I won't hurt her. I'll treasure every shrewish word out of her mouth. I'll protect her as if she were actually sweet and kind. I understand her, and I ask that you hold nothing against my son, Cody. He'll be arriving at Christmas, and we're trying to make a new life together. It's a long shot, but I think it will work. Fiona and I are going to return her little pet, tie up those loose ends, and then I'll bring her safely back here to enjoy the battle. Because—''

"Fiona?" Duncan, Calum, Birk and Elspeth shot at her, worried about Joel's bold claim.

She shivered, Joel's dark jade glance slamming into her senses and raising the hair on her nape. "It's nothing. Really nothing to worry about. I've been in other—''

Joel rounded the counter, trapping her effectively between it and the wall. He looked down at Fiona, who knew that she'd kill him—once her mind, heart and body weren't in shock.

"I'll be bringing her back safely, because of this—'' Joel swept her into his arms and placed his lovely, warm lips on hers as if in slow motion, tasting her, letting her know the shape of his mouth, his scent.

If the kiss had been hard or claiming, she would have destroyed him. But it was filled with heather on the highland mountains and wildflowers in the spring and sunlit honey and butterflies. Beneath simmered a layer of hunger and need that she sensed would match her own.

She flung herself into the kiss, caught his head in both hands and gave her mouth to him, extracting the hot, wild heat. This was what she'd sought, what she wanted, this wild, coming-home heat that settled her, even as it devoured her.

While he was kissing her, Joel had picked her up in his arms. He was just opening the door to leave Hummingbirds when Duncan whispered something, and Joel lifted his lips long enough to say, "Yes. When the time is right, I'll tell her."

Fiona blinked. "I intend to take you apart, piece by piece, you know. I'll destroy you. Let me down."

Joel grinned, a reckless, quick, boyish grin that shocked her. "What a way to go."

He slid her into the seat of the open convertible as easily as if she were a child. Fine. Fiona thought, adjusting herself to the new battle that awaited her—Joel really needed a lesson. Elspeth came running from the shop and handed her the Tallchief plaid, a blanket woven in the design taken from Una's Fearghus clan and altered to add the Tallchief vermillion stripe. "Take this."

Elspeth gently eased Una's chest into Fiona's hands, lingered a moment as Joel slid into the driver's seat and revved the engine. "Aye," Elspeth said quietly, looking at Joel and then at Fiona, who wondered when all her body parts would come to life, and when her fingers would stop trembling and her mouth would stop hungering—

"Aye," Elspeth said again, smoothing Fiona's cropped hair and bending to hug her. "It's time, Fiona the fiery," she whispered. "Fight your lovely battles and come home safe to us. I'll be weaving a new Tallchief plaid."

Fiona glanced at her brothers, lined up beside the car, wearing rosebuds over their ears and glaring at Joel—who looked capable of brawling with them on the spot. Because she wanted the pleasure of ripping Joel Palladin apart herself, Fiona blew her brothers a kiss. A tear glistened on Duncan's hard cheek.

"I'll kill you. You're not up to dealing with my talents," she remarked mildly to the man smoothly gearing the car and leaving Amen Flats.

"I await your pleasure, Princess," he returned grimly.

She flicked him a lazy glance, disguising the energy racing through her, the excitement of battling a worthy, fascinating man. "I'm very good at what I do, Joel. I intend to make you pay. You listened to every single, intimate detail of my—"

"Desires?" he supplied mildly and glanced at her hair. "With the wind riffling your hair, it looks like sleek glossy feathers. It's blue-black and silky and only you could make that bad cut look exotic. It adds to your eyes. I've always liked the shade of smoke and steel. The Celtic headpiece suits you—primitive, intricate and feminine.''

Off balance by his compliments and too furious to speak, Fiona pressed her lips together, still tasting his kiss. She wouldn't talk to him, giving him nothing, until her temper quieted. She wanted to level Joel Palladin, demolish him, but honor demanded that she supply a temporary shot. "Sludge is too good for you.''

He laughed at that, a carefree, boyish laugh that pleased her, and she smothered the smile playing around her lips. He geared down for a sharp curve and reached to take the nape of her neck in one hand, smoothing her skin as if he liked to touch her.

Fiona shook him off and burrowed down into her Tallchief plaid, clutching Una's chest. She intended to take Joel Palladin apart, piece by sizable piece. She would teach him not to dabble in her life.

She longed to dive through the clutter in the chest, but she would do that alone. She wasn't sharing more of her life with Joel Palladin. He already knew more than he should.

She studied the intricate brass buttons on the chest. The only payback for his treachery of listening to her desires and intimate feelings would be to discover his. She intended to drag everything from him and serve it to him on a platter. Then she would walk away.

Pines and sunlight skimmed by her. Mrs. Perkins stopped sweeping her front porch. She stared at Fiona blazing by in the convertible and slowly raised her hand to wave. Mel Morely stopped his tractor and stared. Fiona had the odd feeling that time had skipped back to Tallchief's capture of Una. Fiona sensed that she was a captured bride and that Joel had every intention of keeping her. *To complete the circle, an unlikely love of the battle-maiden will come calling, bringing his angry dragon on one arm and the chest to woo her heart—*

"You have my word that Eunice will be safe and that Palladin, Inc. will stand behind the sale of her to a caring home,'' Joel said quietly as Fiona stood within the curl of Eunice's trunk, hugging her. The front gates of the zoo were securely locked at three o'clock in the morning, and the guard was taking his one-hour break, according to Fiona.

Against the elephant's size, Fiona's body—dressed in a skin-tight black outfit—looked fragile and feminine.

Clouds provided shelter from moonlight, and the trees lining the street added a protective screen. Joel glanced up at the street-light that he'd expertly disabled with a rock. He ran his hand through his hair; he'd shocked himself—Palladin, Inc.'s Iron Man showing off for a woman. Two nights in the vicinity of Fiona Tallchief had rattled him; she was unlike any woman he'd ever known—more feminine and fascinating than he had imagined.

Joel inhaled the cold, crisp air and studied the woman wrapped in the elephant trunk. She was crying softly, smoothing Eunice with her hands, comforting the elephant. He looked down at his boots, unused to the tenderness running through him. He didn't like feeling guilty, and Fiona's silence on the trip added to that weight.

Suddenly Eunice's trunk swept out, caught him and gathered him close to Fiona. Tears glistened on her lashes and on her cheeks. She looked up at him and for the moment her barriers were down, and a very feminine, desirable woman needed him—not in a sexual way, but for the tenderness one heart gives another.

He'd teethed on brutality and shielded himself with calluses. He didn't know if tenderness existed in him—

Iron Man Palladin went down like a load of bricks, awkwardly taking Fiona in his arms. He kissed her lids and gave her what he could, unused to sharing himself with anyone. There was the warmth of her lips, the perfect fit of her body against his—

Fiona pushed him away and dashed the tears from her cheeks with the swipe of her forearm. "You're awfully experienced at break-ins, cutting the headlamps as you came near the zoo. And you looked hard, determined, as if you knew exactly what had to be done. You considered and disabled that streetlight with the air of a surgeon dissecting a gallbladder. You had experienced criminal written all over you, Joel. If anything happens to her, I'll kill you," she promised, urging Eunice to the tall, wrought iron fence. "Up, Eunice."

Eunice promptly extended her trunk, and Fiona stepped on it. He hadn't told Fiona how close to being a criminal he was, or that his father had killed her parents. He wanted time to circle Fiona and to gently serve her that tidbit. Joel held his breath, watching her, and wondered why he was letting her play this dangerous game, when he could have used Palladin, Inc.'s power to—

Fiona stepped onto a solid tree branch above the iron fence, lowered herself, and dropped down behind. In seconds the gate swung open and Eunice lumbered through it as though she was glad to be home. Joel was left to follow. Fiona glanced at him, and they pulled the gates closed. "You'll have to help me over the brick wall for the large animal enclosure. Eunice doesn't like it and—"

She placed her foot into the cup Joel had made with his hands. He levered her up. She pulled herself part of the way and got caught in the shrubs. "Joel...Joel?" she asked in a hushed tone.

He placed one hand on her bottom, while the other pulled away the shrub. He enjoyed the softness braced upon his palm and tilted his head to study the curve of her breasts. "I suppose now would be as good a time as any to tell you that you are the new owner of Eunice."

She stopped struggling, and with one leg up on the top of the wall and her bottom in Joel's two hands, she looked down at him. "What?"

"Your name is on her ownership papers, and the zoo has agreed to take care of her until you find a satisfactory home for her. You might think about Amen Flats. Palladin, Inc. could use the good exposure and would donate a hefty amount to start the ball rolling. It would make an appealing tax deduction. Shut your mouth, darling," he added, amused by her look.

His hand smoothed her bottom, and he held his breath, releasing his tension slowly, controlling the fear that Fiona would hate him even more violently than she had at the funeral. Joel braced himself for what he must do. "You really are very soft...and by the way, my father was the one responsible for killing your parents. When you were ten and running wild after your parents' service, you told me to get off Tallchief Mountain. My brothers and I came to pay our respects and were too late for the church service."

"You!" Her face was starkly revealing, eyes huge in the night, and reminding him of that ten-year-old racked with grief. "You look like him! Palladin...that is the name. I had forgotten—"

"Joel Palladin at your service," he stated, sounding cool, despite the emotions boiling in him. His father's legacy had reached out to cloak Joel in ice.

Fiona hefted herself up to the brick wall, stood and braced her legs apart. She looked down at him, hands on her waist. "What are you doing in my life, Joel Palladin?"

He should have expected the bold question, shot at him like a steel-tipped arrow. He sent the answer back to her, sparing her nothing. "I couldn't forget you, that child on the mountain, and I felt guilty. I knew exactly what you all would have to face to stay together. My brothers and I had been fighting that battle since our mother died and Nick was only six months old. Dad—my father—sold Nick and Rafe. Mamie, my grandmother, would have none of it. She got them back and he kept us, if that's what you could call it, and we came to the mountain that day because we had to. We had to say we were sorry. Pride had to begin somewhere, and we decided we weren't living without it anymore."

He would remember her forever, standing there in the shadows, the wind riffling her hair, her fists tightly balled at her taut thighs. He could feel the emotions humming off her, and for a moment bitterness and raw pain boiled inside him. "I'm not my father, Fiona," he said quietly, because he had to say the words to her, to make her understand. *I've tried so hard not to be.*

He inhaled slowly, forcing the night air into his lungs. He'd never released emotions; how could he really know if he was like his father?

She dropped from sight and pushed open the gates a heartbeat later. Eunice wandered through them, and Fiona shot him a look as they hurried to follow the elephant lumbering to her appropriate enclosure.

"Aye and blast!" Fiona muttered as she stared at the metal chain looped around the gate to Eunice's quarters and fastened with a padlock.

Joel took one look and removed his wallet. A thin foil packet fell to the ground, gleaming like hard evidence of his desire as Fiona shook her head. "That will never happen," she said.

"I'm one of those always-prepared guys," Joel murmured as he extracted a small tool and neatly picked the lock. He'd lied, the purchase was his first in years and was made at a stop for truck fuel after an entire night of Fiona sleeping in the back of the cab...moaning sensually and sleeping, he corrected. Joel had liked the feel of her beside him in bed, in his arms, and he fully intended to snare Fiona for their mutual enjoyment. The purchase of protection was no light matter for him; he never bought anything without a specific purpose, and his body told him that with Fiona, he had distinct goals in their relationship.

Eunice turned and looked at them, as if saying, "I know, guys. You'll do your best for me. I love you."

Her trunk swayed out and ran over Fiona gently, reassuringly. Then Eunice swept Joel against her. "I can't be all bad," he murmured, shaken by the embrace.

"Hmm. She's easy." Fiona's tone was skeptical as she worked quickly, locking the gates behind them. Outside the front gate, Fiona tapped him on the shoulder and said, "It's been fun," as she turned to leave.

"Oh, no, you don't." Joel caught her in two strides, eased her over his shoulder and ran back to the truck, dumping her in the cab. He started the motor and eased the truck down the street and onto another one, before turning on the headlights. "We're taking this back to your friend Danny, and then we're heading home."

Home. He liked the warm curl of the word around him. The woman who sat with folded arms and a petulant expression was not warm.

"I own an elephant, do I? How did I manage that?"

"We have ways, all of them legal and without a jail sentence attached." Joel followed the point of her finger to an off-ramp.

"Palladin, Inc. ways? You know how I dislike the abuse of power and money."

"You're doing this for Eunice, remember? This way, you have personal approval of anyone who wants to own her, you have the option to do something great for Amen Flats, and to top it off, you're innocent of any crime.''

Joel glanced at Fiona, disturbed by his need to protect her. "Just how close are you to Danny?"

"We're very, very friendly." Her smug, intimate smile set him simmering. Jealousy wasn't on his familiar-emotions list, startling him. She reached in back, grabbed her backpack, laden with Una's chest, swung her Tallchief plaid around her shoulders and put her hand on the door handle. "Don't wait for my call."

She glanced down when she heard the click on her wrist. "Handcuffs. How common, but I'd expect something like that from you—shackling me to you."

"I made your family a promise that I intend to keep. I'm bringing you back safely."

"Yawn," she drawled as if the thought bored her. "You'll never make it."

"Won't I?" Joel took her hand, being careful of the metal, so as not to hurt her as they eased from the cab. He hoisted his black leather bag in one hand and held her hand as they walked down the street toward a phone booth.

A half hour later, Joel tossed his bag in the back of the shiny, new, black pickup. He signed the delivery and ownership papers on the salesman's clipboard.

"I should have known," Fiona muttered as she slid into the cab moments later. "I suppose this black monster is the equivalent of the macho medieval charger."

Joel couldn't resist her petulant, tired, feminine snit. He cupped the nape of her neck and took her mouth gently, enjoying the shape and feel of it. "Why don't you snuggle down on my shoulder and sleep?"

"That will be the day," she murmured after a yawn. "You're not getting away with this, and I'm not done with you, Joel Palladin."

She wanted revenge for her parents' murder. Joel glanced at her. The light from the dashboard sent shadows from her lashes upon her cheek. "I am sorry for what my father did, Fiona," he said quietly, meaning it.

"That's another story. He's not a part of this. You should

know, Joel, that I don't like being pushed into corners, and when I'm pushed, I can be very, very bad.'' She gathered her plaid around her, hugging Una's chest close. She settled down on the seat beside him with the ease of a woman who caught sleep where she could find it.

Joel noted the highway signs that would take him back across Kansas, and found Fiona's hand. He slid his fingers against her slender ones, testing the fit, and drew their hands to his thigh.

That's another story, she'd said. At the moment she wasn't condemning him for being the son of a murderer, and few women in her position would have dismissed that fact.

Five

"Aye and blast!" Fiona muttered as she flopped back on her single brass bed, hers since childhood. Her homey, cluttered apartment offered none of the excitement she experienced with Joel. "There isn't another man who can tango like Joel Palladin can, and the jerk knows it."

On a Saturday night, Fiona could have been with any of her family or at Maddy's Hot Spot Tavern. She eased to her side, furious with Joel for keeping her from another night's sleep. She hadn't seen him since he'd dropped her off at her apartment early last Sunday morning as if... Fiona scowled at the fresh-cut calla lilies standing in her mother's elegant cut-glass vase and spoke aloud, "As if I hadn't made an impact on his life."

The graceful sway of his body, the heat and motion of corded muscles—a man who knew what to do with a woman in his arms haunted her. On the way back to Amen Flats, he'd drawn women's glances at every café, every stop for gas. A tango had come on the jukebox just as they were leaving a café, and without missing a beat, Joel had swept Fiona into his arms and tangoed her in the space between tables. The challenge of the taut Latin American dance was too much for her to resist.

Joel, she brooded, knew every intricate move and step, playing the dominating male as he dynamically molded their bodies together and flowed with the Latin beat, whipping Fiona around as if he owned her. The problem was—the impromptu dance delighted her. The people in the restaurant clapped, and with Fiona bent back over his arm, he had kissed her until she'd clung to him, wanting more. "If you were interested in me," he'd said, "you would ask questions. But since you're in a snit and acting like a clam, I'll tell you that I worked as a dance instructor at night. Women seemed to like me for some reason. Of course, none of them ever told me that she was a very ready virgin. I'll be very careful with you, darling," he'd whispered, one hand caressing her back.

"'A very ready virgin.' Aye and blast!" Fiona repeated. The bed creaked as she flipped over onto her stomach. She traced the sewing chest's stick figures of a man and a woman and Tallchief Mountain, then opened it to prowl through the beloved contents. She went through them lightly, sensing that other women had cherished the contents and had added to it, giving bits of their loves and lives. There was a fine thread for making lace, a spinning top with a metal point and the colors worn through to the wood, colored swatches of woven wool, as if some weaver wanted to remember the color. The tatting shuttle, ivory crochet hooks and a shoe button hook gleamed. The coins were very old, and the buttons were of deer horn and intricate Celtic design on brass. An awl, used to make holes in leather, had the stick figures on the handle, and Fiona imagined Tallchief etching them with his knife. Tatted lace was wrapped around a piece of horn, and Fiona traced the lace, slowly unwinding it.

A tiny folded paper, turned yellow with age, fell to the quilt. When Fiona gently opened it, a woman's handwriting curved delicately upon the paper:

I am all alone in the wilds, with no family to comfort me, and so I share my thoughts with papers. I love Tallchief, the rogue, and he knows it. He knows I want him with my body, that the fever is upon me when he but touches me. I am not alone in the fever, for I see it in Tallchief's eyes, each time that black, fierce gaze holds me...when heat flashes and burns away his cold heart. Yet I will not bend to his will, nor will I be ordered about like his captive. I cannot give my body and keep my heart apart. Nor can I give my heart to a man wanting only my body. He thinks he will have me without the tenderness that a man must give a woman. He thinks that he is a mighty dragon, my swaggering chieftain-laird, while I am to do his bidding. I will have what I need. What every woman needs. Deep in the corners of my fierce heart, I long for the battle and the love.

Una

Fiona imagined her great-great-grandmother, lifting her Scots chin, her gray eyes warring with the tall chieftain, who desired her. "I don't think love will come to me, Una," Fiona whispered, giving way to the shadows that were never far from her. "I've been looking for a long time...hoping, too. And I've certainly dated enough. Though I've had good friends, I just couldn't bear to think that any of those men could touch me intimately. My last date called me 'frigid.' I've begun to wonder if I am. Or at least, if my sensuality is low."

She laughed nervously. "Now that was quite an admission from someone who hasn't cared about anything but rebelling against the establishment."

Her parents' love was perfect, laughter and love running between them like sunlight. They blended, in Fiona's mind, one running into the other, loving the other.

"I'm too independent, Una. I don't like restrictions of any kind. Like you, I'm not certain I can share myself, not the deepest heart of me." Fiona tried on the horsehair ring, tapping the blue beads. The smaller ring was definitely Una's, and a larger ring had belonged to Tallchief. She remembered reading about them in Una's journals.

Fiona skimmed the flat of her hand over the old quilt made by her grandmother LaBelle, a world-class cat burglar...until grandfather Jake turned up at her fancy soiree to claim her.

Fiona's reaction to Joel was just body heat and basic sexual survival, Fiona mulled the thought and the restless ache in her body. "I guess I'm not exactly frigid."

She picked up the intricately woven brass headband and remembered how Joel's eyes had flashed, brilliant as dark emeralds, when he'd placed it upon her. There was definite male ownership in his expression, when he directed it toward her. She didn't know if she liked that tether; she'd escaped it for years.

Joel had no deep love or tenderness in him, except when he spoke of his son. She could count on Joel not to ask more of her emotionally than she could give. Joel was "Not an asker," she stated aloud. "But he might be just the perfect candidate to see what's making me so restless. He doesn't appear to want emotional ties, which means I could leave the relationship when I wanted. I'd like that option."

She flopped to her back and traced the brass designs on her footboard with her toe. Joel had been busy she knew, ordering lumber and hauling plumbing fixtures and scouring the countryside for old furniture that suited him. His black truck-monster slid by her shop window at least once a day. Meanwhile he'd forgotten her.

No male had ever forgotten Fiona Tallchief; she devastated them and walked away.

Eunice was safe and well tended, according to Danny. Amen Flats was thrilled with the prospect of a new zoo and the hefty donation from Palladin, Inc. By spring Eunice would have a brand-new home in Amen Flats.

Joel Palladin kissed like hot sin, covered by soft dreamy silk. His backside was made for tight-fitting jeans, and shoulders like his were made for a woman's head to rest upon. Fiona frowned; she had never thought about resting her head against any man's shoulder, she'd been too busy pushing through life and blazing environmental, animal and humanity trails. When Joel watched Fiona with those dark, knowing eyes, her flesh heated and tingled and she wanted to feast upon him.

Fiona arched slowly, restlessly, sensuously upon the hand-stitched quilt. She needed to clear the battlefield for the war; and when the war was finished, she'd walk away from Joel and he from her.

She glanced at the ringing telephone and picked it up. "Whoever you are, you're one of my brothers. Elspeth is too shrewd to be foraging in my life," Fiona tossed into the receiver and smiled at the long pause. For the last week, her brothers had hovered over her. "It's Duncan," she stated after a moment, a smile curling on her lips. "And you're worried."

He cleared his throat, apparently uneasy as she went right to the reason for his call. "We were just going down to Maddy's and thought you might want to join us."

Fiona stroked the tiny brass flowers on an intricate Celtic brooch. "I've got things to do."

After delivering Una's chest, flashing his dragon and dragging her off like a warrior claiming his bride, Joel had unceremoniously dumped her. She'd been prepared to kiss him, devastate him, because she'd never truly tried the famed Tallchief kiss. According to Amen Flats' gossip, the Tallchief brothers' lip-sucking, mind-blowing, storm-making kiss, could devastate. Alek, after a surprise session with Elspeth, who was out to teach him a lesson, looked fierce and steaming and hungry.

Fiona tapped her finger on the chest. Joel Palladin deserved payback for abandoning her, and he would never stuff sentimental obligations into her kiss. She could trust him not to be sentimental—Fiona held her breath and plunged on with her thoughts about Joel. She could trust him; Palladin's Iron Man was reputed not to have a heart.

To complete the circle, an unlikely love of the battlemaiden will come calling, baring his angry dragon on one arm— Fiona didn't believe whimsy or Una's legend would involve herself.

Duncan made growling protective noises, informing her that Joel Palladin was not for her. "He's too tough. He'll hurt you," Duncan worried.

"I love you, Duncan. I adore you. But would you kindly keep your nose out of my business? Ask Sybil or Elspeth or Emily if you should interfere and they will tell you the same. Think of it this way—Joel has the dragon on his arm and he brought me Una's chest, and you know how all those legends have come true.

First you, then Calum, then Birk and Elspeth. You'll just have to trust me on this one, brother dear.'' Fiona smiled as she thought of Sybil's daughter, seventeen-year-old Emily, who was drawing boys' attention. Emily was thoroughly frustrated by the protective Black Knights of the Tallchiefs.

"You're all I've got left," he grumbled sadly. "And Palladin is wearing calluses all over him. Your heart is too soft. He'll hurt you."

"Mmm. Think of him as wearing armor. He doesn't scare me, and he's thrown down a challenge that I can't walk away from."

"If you go hunting him, it could be war."

Fiona smoothed the stick figures on the chest. Just as Una wouldn't let Tallchief set the terms, Fiona wouldn't let Joel unravel her. "I intend to win."

Fiona lifted her head to the night wind carrying the scent of pines, coming winter and wood smoke from Joel's house. It was no drab or thoughtless thing she was doing, digging at what ran hot and wild and haunting between Joel Palladin and herself. Those emotions were not whimsy or legends, but real. With the weather storming high on the Rockies, her Tallchief blood was up for prowling and battling and claiming. She let the wind tug at her short hair, and drew the Tallchief plaid closer around her shoulders. Wearing a thick red sweater and a light, flannel-lined jacket and jeans, she needed the Tallchief colors around her more for security than for warmth. Morning Star, her Appaloosa mare that Birk kept in the pasture behind his house, moved smoothly down the hill toward the house.

Fiona whipped the Tallchief plaid over one shoulder. Joel had dared step into her life; he'd made a bold claim. She couldn't let that pass. Or wait for him to come swaggering into her life when he chose. "I've never been a good one to wait."

She would take Joel Palladin apart and leave, reclaiming her pride, her honor.

Joel stepped from the shadows of the porch and stood waiting in the moonlight, watching her as she neared him. She stopped Morning Star in front of him, and Joel stroked the mare's neck, his eyes locked with hers.

"You can't drop me off at my shop like a bouquet of wilted, unwanted flowers," she erupted, when she had planned to assault him coldly, and meticulously tear him apart. "Not after waltzing into my shop, declaring that you'd fight my brothers to get me, and packing me off."

"Ah. You do like protocol. I thought you were too much of a rebel for that," he drawled.

She could feel herself winding up, reveling in the excitement of the coming battle, where she would strip him down to his bones and—

She swung easily to the ground, and Joel narrowed his eyes down at her. "You're all worked up, Fiona the fiery," he noted in a clinical tone. "I wonder why."

"You've been talking to my family. I'll see to them. I won't let them give one piece of me. And you're right, I'm...not exactly happy," she admitted as he took the reins from her and walked Morning Star to the barn. She followed, uncertain now that she had Joel within throttling...or kissing range.

He'd just bathed, his hair still damp and curling at the nape of his neck, and the scent of soap clung to him. The battered gray sweatshirt stretched tautly across his chest, and Fiona wished his outlaw look, the dark and dangerous male, did not appeal to her. He looked...physical. Her senses kicked into high gear, as she remembered telling a Joel she thought was sleeping that she wanted a physical man.

"I suppose you know that each of your brothers has paid me a call, asking my intentions and threatening me."

She waited. Then, because she couldn't wait a heartbeat longer, she asked, "And? Did they frighten you? And what did you say?"

He eased Morning Star into a stall beside his gelding. "That you would have to make the call on what happens between us. But if you wanted me, nothing could stop me from having you, brawling Tallchiefs or not," he answered slowly, turning to her. "Just what are the base rules to this game between you and me?"

Unprepared for the abrupt question, Fiona floundered. Joel's hand smoothed her cheek, his thumb running across her bottom lip. "Be reasonable, Princess. I can't do all the running. I've laid an offer on the table and you're considering it."

"You make it sound so cold." She followed Joel out of the barn and watched him close the doors. "Thank you for Eunice, by the way. It's not every day that a girl gets an elephant for a gift."

"I like Eunice. She's a great hugger. You were right to rescue her. For what it's worth, you've been absolutely right in all of your causes. Even Palladin's contribution to destroying the environment. I took care of that, by the way. Your frog pond is safe, Princess. All those little princes you might want to kiss are on their safe little lily pads. We should make a tidy profit from selling the process." He lifted her tartan plaid, adjusted the fold over one shoulder. Pulling gently on the cloth, Joel brought Fiona closer, his breath sweeping warm on her cold face. "Now why are you here?"

She took a step back, wanting to choose her own time, only to be drawn slowly to Joel. He gently eased a wisp of hair behind her ear. "I won't hurt you, as I've said before. I'll be very careful. But I'm aching for you, and it's been years since I've wanted a woman as badly. Perhaps I have never wanted a woman like I want you, if that's of any use to you. I want to be in you, filling you, moving with you. I'll be very careful that you don't conceive."

While the bold image stunned her, his hand skimmed lightly over her shoulder and down her arm to find her hand. Holding her eyes, he raised the back of her hand to his lips, turned it and placed his face within her keeping. "I don't believe in the fantasy of love—for myself. I suppose the closest I've come to love is with my son, my brothers, and my grandmother. I am not offering you love...I don't know that it is in me, but I won't betray you for the duration, and when we're done, I'll say nothing of what passed between us. We'll both be free. You seem to like your freedom, moving as quickly as you do through life. Would you come into my house?"

The erotic movement of his lips against her palm jarred Fiona. Then Joel walked away and into his house, leaving the door open. No one walked away from Fiona, not in the middle of an important discussion. She put her hands on her waist. Pride demanded that she leave. Curiosity and need caused her to follow.

She closed the door quietly, looking at the wild clutter of boards and saws, crates of new windows and doors, and plumbing fixtures lined against the wall. Crates of new appliances stood in the shadows, clothing tossed over them. On the floor in the living room, a small motor lay in pieces on newspaper, his tools neatly arranged in a perfect line. A makeshift desk—boards placed over sawhorses—was cluttered with a portable computer, a facsimile machine loaded with incoming paper, and an opened suitcase.

Fiona studied the faxes pinned to the wall. Words were misspelled and the numbers across the top of the page were the same—Palladin, Inc. "Nobody with the intelligence of dirt lives on a farm stuck in nowhere. Get back to Denver." Another one read, "Partner, you are not wanted in this part of the corral. Mosey away." The next one was brilliant, "Git. No city people wanted hereabouts." Then there was a classic, "Joel. This is Mamie. Go to Alaska. Get a whale. We need one. Sell your farm."

"My son. He's not exactly happy with me," Joel explained behind Fiona.

"He's obviously creative and is actively fighting what he doesn't like. I like that." She turned to Joel. He stood with his hands in his jeans' back pockets. The bald light bulb overhead emphasized his hard looks, bold cheekbones and the burning of his eyes.

"I remember you that day on the mountain," Fiona said, prowling through time. "The three of you, looking tired and hungry and with eyes that asked for something I didn't understand. I understand the need, but a note would have done just as well. You must have only been seventeen or so. There were holes in your jeans, and your jackets weren't warm enough for the mountain. The wind must have gone straight through you..."

She closed her eyes, remembering that stark, cold day when her parents lay fresh in their graves. "You were city boys and didn't know how to handle the horses."

"We came because of our pride—because of honor. Back then, it was the only thing that kept us from sinking into and following our father's life. Calum has probably investigated all of us by now. He's a top researcher and no doubt protective of his baby sister. I'm certain he can fill in any missing blanks. Our mother died when Nick was only six months old and Rafe a year older. My father promptly...illegally...sold both Nick and Rafe. They were young enough to be wanted. At four, I was already a 'problem child' and not a pretty child to market. My grandmother was furious—'' Joel shifted restlessly, the clean but stained, gray sweatshirt tightening across his chest. He lifted his head, slamming shut the painful door.

She gripped the chair, her fingers aching. Memories of the tall, tough, haunted-looking teenagers curled around Fiona. "You said you knew how hard it would be. That's why you came."

The muscle in Joel's cheek contracted, his skin gleaming and dark. "We knew, and by then we were seasoned at surviving, and we wanted to help...to do anything. Looking back, we should have known our reception wouldn't be exactly warm."

His mouth softened, curling slightly. "There you were, hurtling over the rocks and sliding down a hill, black braids flying, gleaming in the wind. And your face...I'll never forget how fierce you were, standing there with that rock in your hand, yelling—''

Joel shook his head. "Lloyd Palladin ruined your childhood, Fiona. He took it away. And I'm his son. I could be just like him."

The hard admission startled her. She thought back to what Calum's research had told her, how Mamie Palladin, their grandmother, had fought her own son to claim the three neglected boys. "We Tallchief children were loved and cherished and taught to do the same. We played and were well fed, and you probably never had a childhood, Joel. How could you care so much?"

Joel inhaled, the bald light creating shadows from his lashes, softening the jut of his cheekbones. "Because we imagined how it would be to have parents like yours. Because we knew it was worse to have had them and know the feeling, than never to have known it."

"Joel..." Fiona sensed that he'd never told anyone the barren truth about his life, pride keeping him quiet. "Joel, you and your brothers had nothing to do with your father's actions."

"We knew. But it didn't help. Is his murder of your parents going to be a problem between us?"

She knew he'd faced her brothers, asked them the same question, and each had repeated it to her, a warning. Her brothers did not hold Joel accountable. They knew how difficult her childhood had been, the strict relentless goals and rules she'd set for herself that went against her wild, battling nature.

"You visited Elspeth and asked her that question. What did she say?" Fiona asked, because Elspeth alone had been too quiet since the day Joel had swept her away.

"She said that sometimes she knew too much and she had weaving to do. Over a cup of peppermint tea, and while Heather, her baby, was giving me jam kisses and investigating my ear, Elspeth said that dragons had always fallen to the magic of circles. She said that you could be 'difficult and dangerous' were her terms, and that you would pick your time. Have you picked your time, Fiona?"

"Why do you want me?" Fiona asked in a whisper, uncertain of her emotions, aching for Joel the teenager, and wary of Joel the man. She had to know the truth and if he—

"Heat. You make me feel heat. I'm alive with you, and I'm definitely not bored," he said simply, watching her. "Then there's ordinary lust. It developed quite sharply when you got my attention by dumping sludge over my head. I've been tracking your causes for years. You made a difference, Fiona, a big one. And I knew when you were tired and wanted more. I knew because I've had that hollow ache most of my life."

She tossed away her sympathy for Joel the teenager and lifted her chin. Joel as an adult was another matter. "Calum said you'd changed your mind about a temporary stay for your son's sake, and you've got permanent plans to stay, city boy...that you'd resigned your position at Palladin's, except for consulting, and that you are serious about becoming a rancher. This is a tough land and not for the inexperienced. Why are you here?"

"You want it all, don't you?" Joel turned slowly toward the school picture braced on a small shelf. Cody resembled his father, from dark brown waving hair to green eyes and the cleft in his chin. "For him. Maybe for me. I believed his mother, Patrice, my ex-wife, because she came from a good family and good parents. I believed Cody when he told me everything was fine and that he didn't want to see me. Everything wasn't fine, and his mother doesn't want him any longer...she just didn't want me to have him."

Joel straightened the picture, running his finger over the boy's face in a caress. "Mamie thought the same about us, that we were getting care. My father cleaned us up before her visits, and kids can be bought to lie with promises. I should have known better with Cody. I want to give him what I can. Cody has always wanted a ranch and animals, and there's something I want, too—something I've built with my bare hands and claimed."

Joel's gaze drifted around the old house, cluttered with tools and warm with shadows of others. "You grew up one way, on Tallchief land...I grew up another and in several places. Now I want this. Between Cody and me, we might make it work."

Pain shifted through Joel's dark expression before he closed his thoughts away. She sensed that he'd given her more than he'd given anyone, a concession she hadn't expected.

Fiona ran her fingertips over the old rosebud wallpaper, which was brighter where the Watkins family pictures had been. He loved Cody enough to try rebuilding a homestead that could defeat a seasoned rancher.

Honor. It ran through Joel like steel, and Fiona knew that he would keep his word.

An excellent researcher, Calum had told her that Joel had been tagged Palladin's Iron Man, a man without emotions. Yet they ran deep in him, pain flashing in his expression as he talked about his son, his voice softening. Joel would not leave his son alone as Lloyd Palladin's sons had been, foraging for food and shelter on the street. Joel had kept two younger brothers warm and fed, when he could easily have left them. "You're bringing your son here, because you want him to experience Amen Flats, small-town America and neighbors who care, don't you?"

"Something like that." His answer was too curt, and she knew she had him, his defenses were up. Joel closed the top of his laptop, the click sounding final in the quiet shadows.

Fiona glanced into the old sewing room, where she had shared so many hours with Mrs. Watkins. If she had a child who needed a home, safety and a fence against the forces that could ruin his life, she would do exactly what Joel intended. He had honor, so she admired him, and in the time she'd known him, he had not lied to her. She had simply jumped to her own conclusions, and she would have to be wary of that in the future. Fiona swept around the table laden with tools, needing to put something between them, her nerves humming.

"Where did you get Una's chest?" she shot at him, wanting to know everything at once.

"I don't think I want to go into the details of that just yet," Joel stated, glancing at the two kittens stretching and yawning and tumbling from a low cardboard box. "Meet my up-and-coming barn cats, Mix and Match. Mix is the calico and Match is the gray."

Delighted with the tiny balls of fur, Fiona tossed her plaid over a chair and knelt to play with them. Joel crouched beside her. His hand skimmed her hair, and when she looked up at him, Joel's expression was almost tender as he said, "Stay with me, Fiona. Lie in my bed with me, and tell me what happened to you. How hard it was to be good all those years, saving yourself for me."

Fiona studied Joel's expression, dissecting it. It lay between desire, mockery of himself and whimsy. She dismissed whimsy; it wasn't on the Palladin Iron Man's customary menu. "I don't like rules or orders, and you're full of them. I saw your office...you're structured—a minus in your account, much too neat, analytical and methodical in getting what you want—another minus. Logic isn't one of my favorite games. Sometimes you can miss a real opportunity by trying to think it out, so I trust my impulses. And you're used to getting your way—a definite minus, because I like having mine. I don't promise to be good with you," she returned slowly.

His finger circled her ear, tugging gently on the tiny, dangling moss agate earring. "With me, Fiona the fiery, I expect you to be very bad and very honest."

"We have that between us, I suppose—honesty." She gave him an arch look and cuddled the kittens close to her. "You didn't have to tell me your feelings, yet you gave them to me."

He hadn't told her everything. The dark shadows clung to him as he rubbed Mix under the chin, and Match batted at his finger.

"What do you need?" he asked Fiona in an uneven, deep whisper that skittered along her skin and into her heart.

"That you always be honest with me in return."

"I can give you that," he spoke firmly as if giving his pledge.

"You're not so tough, Joel Iron Man Palladin. Or you wouldn't have fallen for both kittens. One would do for a barn cat. They are old enough to be kept in the barn now, not where you can pet them and stuff them with expensive kitty food," she whispered as his mouth came softly, warmly over her parted one.

She lingered, enjoying the light, tantalizing brush of his lips for a moment and placed her hand on his arm, claiming his dragon. "You know too much about me, Mr. Palladin, while I know little about you. I intend to—"

"You know the essentials." His tongue flicked against her bottom lip. "I expect you will have a thorough investigation of me done soon. You're like that—meticulous about your involvements. You want me, and you're going to have me in your own time and in what you think are your own terms."

"Will I? Don't be so certain," she whispered, temper simmering. She kissed the kittens before she handed them to him. Joel was too confident, arrogant, while she was shaking. She stood, reached for her plaid and said, "Don't call me, I'll—"

Joel placed the kittens near their milk and stood slowly. "No, you won't," he said, tugging her into his arms. He flicked off the light switch behind her, and with her feet above the floor, he simply carried her to his bed.

This is what I want, Fiona thought wildly as Joel's solid body covered hers. *What I need.*

"I'm not fighting you," she whispered as Joel's lips nibbled at hers.

He chuckled and eased out of his sweatshirt, then burrowed his face against the hollow of her throat and shoulder. "No, you're not fighting me. But you haven't decided to enter the game just yet, have you? You're weighing all the gives and takes and forging your battle plan, aren't you? You're wondering how much of your independence you'll have to give and what I'll take and what you can get from me. I like that, the dissecting of reality, cutting away fantasy. Few women are capable of keeping their emotions reined. You say you're impulsive, but there's a fine, intricate, feminine mind ticking inside this." He kissed her temple.

Then Joel eased to her side, placed his arms over his head and grinned at her. "I've missed the scent of you, like bluebells and heather in the mountain wind. That and the woman scent... You may leave now, or I can tell you how I want to put my hands on you, tend your breasts and kiss them and make them stop aching—"

Fiona narrowed her eyes. "You're no gentleman, Palladin. I thought you were sleeping when I said that."

Then, because he grinned as if he'd gotten the best of her, she lowered her lips to his chest, flicked his nipple with her tongue.

"Is this what you want, Fiona the fiery?" he asked, hauling her up to him, his expression fierce and demanding as he placed his mouth over hers.

She would take him and be done, keeping her heart safe—she would have no rule maker stepping inside her emotions—

His hands were trembling, rough textured against her stomach, flowing lightly beneath her sweater, coming to rest upon her breasts. His caress was so gentle, seeking the shape of her beneath her bra, cupping her.

She hadn't expected to feel so soft, so feminine and yielding. So treasured.

She hadn't known the beauty of being gently, so reverently touched as if she were priceless. Magic, the woman inside her thought, warming...he touches me and magic happens. She hadn't expected the storm of emotions, rather the quick burning of her body—

"Sweetheart," Joel whispered longingly, unevenly, the old-fashioned endearment curling around her, pleasuring her because it was just for her, just as Joel was meant for her.

Lace tore and she waited for his hands to come upon her. They came slowly, trembling and gentle, despite their calluses, size and weight, and she cried out with the exquisite pleasure, tears burning her lids, and one sliding slowly down her cheek.

Joel's slow enticing kisses brushed her lips and crossed her cheek. He held very still, his body trembling as he slowly raised to look down at her face. He looked angry and yet sad, disappointed, his hair standing out in peaks from her fingers. His hands slid slowly away, tugging down her sweater.

"What happened?" she asked unevenly, shaken by his expression.

He'd taken himself away, though he lay next to her, his forearm over his face, a shudder racking his body.

How could he leave her now with the magic still floating, heating inside her, the song unsung?

Sweetheart, he'd whispered, desperately, and she'd treasured the uneven, rasping sound of his deep voice...*and now he was done with her?*

Anger and frustration surged out of her like a wild beast. She hadn't been skilled enough.

Fiona leaped out of bed, shaking badly. Wrapping her pride and dignity around her, she lifted her head. "I am not a happy woman, Palladin."

Six

Joel yanked on the crowbar harder than necessary, his body humming with the needs Fiona had ignited hours before. The hardwood board he had intended to replace in the old kitchen broke, the crack echoing in the night. The violence shimmered elegantly in his glass of wine and the candles set upon the floor.

Violence. He'd teethed on it. Perhaps he was his father's son, inheriting a primitive need to dominate, to take and claim a woman. He'd shown Fiona how hungry he was for her, and he'd taken her mouth with passion driving him. She'd answered him with her own hungers. And sometime in the fever that hunger had feathered into temptation, to softness—

After arriving two weeks ago, working night and day until he dropped into bed, Joel had replaced the old well pump with a new one. He was surprised at how much he enjoyed tinkering with the equipment, the tools in his hands and the motor purring successfully. He'd attended to the various permits he needed, and with the aid of a plumber, had hot and cold running water and a toilet. The new thermal windows were installed and the outside doors refinished with new storm doors. The old wood cookstove was in the kitchen, because he couldn't bear to part with it. He had everything he needed to keep his son warm in Wyoming's fierce winter, including a new, efficient woodstove and baseboard heaters in every room.

A new facsimile paper curled out of the machine, the purchase of a new restaurant chain needing his attention. Doug Michaels, Joel's protégé and replacement, was capable, recognizing problems beyond his experience, but needed Joel's consultation. Joel had a place for his son; modern-day science allowed him to protect Mamie's empire, small repayment for what she had done for him and his brothers.

"I have everything I need," Joel stated grimly while easing the broken board out of the floor and replacing it.

Except Fiona in his bed.

He hadn't meant to let himself dive into the soft warmth of her, in a whimsical beckoning that had drawn him to no other woman. He hadn't meant to kiss her desperately, ripping away the shields of his hunger, exposing his need of her.

The tenderness erupting in him had frightened him.

Though it had been years since he'd had a woman, he remembered the cold, clinical way he'd satisfied her and himself. Was that sex really satisfying, or a temporary release without the heat?

She wouldn't like rules, and he had made a life of them, structuring a wall against the invasion of his emotions. The potential for jealousy, a new emotion, surprised him.

Joel studied his hands, which could easily have left bruises on her smooth skin. He detested men who were violent with women.

What made him want to share his thoughts with Fiona? He'd been able to tuck women in neat compartments before.

Her tear had stopped him...just one drop of moisture, a silvery trail of dampness down her soft cheek...more effective than Mamie standing over the bed.

Joel threw down the crowbar and wiped the sweat from his face. "Well, fine," he said to Mix and Match who were tumbling, racing, swatting each other around the living room furniture. "So last Saturday night, I'm gallant—God knows where that came from—and on Monday, I'm aching to hear her voice, so I pick up the phone and order flowers for Mamie. It's Saturday night

again, and Miss Tallchief has until Monday to put in an appear-
ance or—''

Exactly how did he make himself appealing to a woman who
wanted nothing more to do with him. He'd gripped the phone,
waiting for one warm word from her, damn her, her wildflower
scent curling around him. Fiona had been curt, businesslike and
shutting any doors to further conversation. His pride demanded
that he not call again; he would simply—what? He listened to the
sound of a horse stopping, the creak of leather, and footsteps
stalking across the porch.

The front door slammed as though someone was sharing his
bad temper, and Joel sat in the shadows, his back braced against
the wall. Fiona, dressed in tight black jeans and her warm tartan
plaid covering her black, long-sleeved sweater, stepped into the
doorway of the kitchen. Her hair had been ruffled by wind, and
she stood, legs braced apart, looking down at him and tapping a
fat envelope on her thigh.

In an effort to seem calm, while his body was already hardening, lurching at her scent, Joel picked up his wineglass, swirled
the contents and sipped slowly.

"You're looking dark and broody," she noted pleasantly. She
tossed a fat envelope onto his lap and dismissed his lack of welcome. "I think we're even now. I've discovered that you've had
me investigated thoroughly, and I repaid the favor. That's your
juvenile record—somewhat altered, according to the date
gaps—the dance studios where you worked while putting yourself
through college, the truck loading docks, some news articles,
where you were born, the different places you lived before Mamie's acquisition of your family, information on your brothers,
and it appears that someone did a real cleanup job...I would suppose you had a hand in it."

"Mamie handled several unsavory items. It didn't matter to
me. I'd already lived it." Joel braced himself against the darkness
she had found. While he'd been hungering for her, he'd been a
fool to think that Fiona would dismiss the past. "Then you know
my father was killed in prison. I suppose Calum is very thorough,
investigating me, or Sybil has. I've seen their work."

"This is my work, Palladin. I'm not exactly the baby you think

I am...all those causes were carefully researched, you know. I know your father's aliases and how, immediately after he was taken captive by my brothers, those three boys who came to the mountain suddenly dropped from sight. Mamie did a good job, I'd say, turning your lives around...and that's what you intend to do with Cody."

Fiona glanced around the room, and entranced, Joel watched her face soften as she noted the old sewing room. "The light in there is perfect for plants. I used to crochet with Mrs. Watkins, or weave. My mother used to say that when a woman weaves, she's putting her heart into it, settling the world and troubles and—"

Fiona broke off and began again. "In the spring you'll see Mrs. Watkins' wonderful flower garden, or what's left of it. No one has tended the bulbs for years, separating them. I used to love the brilliant yellow border of daffodils against that old picket fence."

She turned back to Joel. "I'm good at what I do, and from the facts, I'd say you're making an extraordinary effort to save your son. You don't want him to step into the life you had—aye and blast you," she shot at him. "You're the one who scooped Una's chest from Sybil's grasp, just as she had made connection with the owners and was set to travel, to verify it. Someone matching your description arrived too quickly and offered the owners an ungodly sum and strolled away with it. He had a cleft in his chin and according to her—wicked, delightful green eyes. She said he reminded her of a boy making off with a pirate's chest, when it was only old lace and costume jewelry. He strolled away whistling, she said."

She pushed back the black, glossy hair feathering her cheek. "It wasn't fair to seduce the woman with your charm, Joel...to make off with the chest while an eighty-year-old woman is swooning over your bad-boy looks, and serving you cookies and milk. Take a memo, old chum, your methods of persuasion won't work on me."

Fiona took a deep breath, whipped off her tartan plaid and folded it precisely, concentrating on it as if she were preparing for battle. Joel eased to his feet and braced himself; he would stand when she dismissed him. He'd expected her investigation of him; Fiona was a fastidious, intelligent woman, picking her way through what she wanted. The facts, stacked against him, said that she wouldn't want him.

"So you've come to claim me then," he said, challenging her, sensing that she was prepared to end whatever ran between them.

Her head went up, eyes cutting at him like steel, her body taut. He saw her then, poised in the wind, at home in the wild mountain elements, pride in the lift of her head, the set of her shoulders. She would stand the test of time and troubles.

"Aye and blast. I have, Joel Palladin. I suppose it's the blasted temporary reckoning between us, or because I'm a Tallchief and October raises my wild emotions. You had no right to be gallant, to pull away from me because of a teardrop. You looked as stricken as one of my brothers when a woman cries. I don't think of you as my brother, Joel Palladin, understand that. The tear came of its own will, because your hands upon my breasts created a lovely warm weight."

The beauty of her words slammed into him; he wasn't expecting the softness from her.

She took the wineglass from him, lifted and drained it. While he foraged through how to handle this volatile woman, Fiona stated, "You're afraid of me, Joel. You don't know how to handle me. Admit it."

He inhaled, jarred by the desirable female challenging him. He'd always controlled his emotions; he would now. "Don't push, Fiona."

"I know who you are, Joel Palladin. Deep inside where you dream of romance and fantasy and dragons slaying the wrong-doers. I've got brothers and they quiver at a tear, just like you." She trailed her fingertip around his jaw, placed it in the cleft of his chin and smirked. "Lovely. Just lovely. Palladin's Iron Man runs for the bushes at a virgin's tear.... And by the way, I really did not appreciate you investigating my past few boyfriends' credit cards and the motels they visited. Affairs don't really require double beds. Once I tapped into your private electronic service, the rest was a piece of cake. You've made me your hobby, Palladin. Now I've made you mine. If you want to know whose bed I slept in, it was my own. Goodbye, Palladin,'' she added lightly, then picked up her plaid on her way out and slammed the door behind her.

She ran on foot through the night, ducking pine branches over the trail and muttering, Morning Star's reins clasped in her hand. Joel Palladin had raised her fears and her longings and he could tear her apart. His vulnerability, longing to give his son a meaningful life, and his tenderness would have sunk any woman's defenses. Fiona ducked a branch, hopped over a log and leaped into panic. Sweat dripped from her, impatiently swept away, only to return. Her heart raced, pounded with running and with the thoughts of how Joel had looked, towering over her, a man no longer cold and hard, but one steaming and hungry.

"He made me break one of my rules—going after him as though he needed to be claimed! As if I were running after him! I've actually cooked and cleaned for that man, and worried about him!''

After returning Morning Star to Birk's pasture, Fiona walked through the familiar shadows of Amen Flats. There was Calum and Talia's house, a modern affair; Lacey and Birk's restored bordello stood on a knoll overlooking Amen Flats. Near Tallchief Mountain, Duncan and Sybil and their brood nestled in their beds, and Elspeth and Alek cherished the old Russian homestead with sheep grazing in the moonlit fields. Fiona studied the mountains jutting into the night sky, calling her. Perhaps her Tallchief blood sang wild in the night, the trees and the rocks and the meadows beckoning to her.

This was home and where she had to find herself. Fiona let herself into the greenhouse, needing the fresh earth scents and the cool ferns brushing at her hot cheeks. Abe and George, lizards that kept her greenhouse free of insect pests, hurried along the cool tile floor, peering up at her.

Fiona shivered, sweeping the flat of her hand along the heather starts as she moved through the darkness. In the spring she and Elspeth would plant the starts on Tallchief Mountain where their parents could enjoy them. At one o'clock in the morning she wanted Joel Palladin's lean and muscular, slightly hairy, warm and desirable body curled around her. "Without a stitch between us," Fiona added her thought aloud.

Perhaps she had inherited her wild needs from Tallchief, the need to claim Joel Palladin humming through her like a taut, hot wire that wouldn't let her rest.

She reached the showcase, surveyed the flowers and selected tiny, white, tea rosebuds, braiding them with baby's breath and ferns and placing the delicate coronet on top of her head. Years ago her mother used to braid sweetgrass and wildflowers and— Fiona sighed heavily, tiredly, accepting the sleepless hours ahead of her until the shop opened in the morning. Because she needed more soothing, Fiona scooped up the display of lush red roses and buried her face in their fragrance.

She'd been obsessed by her investigation of Joel's life, and now that it was over, she was even more fascinated with him than before. She'd made him angry, his body tense and his face angular, hard, eyes riveting hers while Mozart framed their duel with music.

Fiona tiredly tugged off her boots, dropping them on her way to the staircase leading to her room. She tossed the roses onto her bed, because she intended to wallow in them for comfort, saving the thorns for one Joel Palladin. She slid off her sweater, eased off her bra and shimmied out of her jeans and panties.

The shower water, sluicing over her, did little to calm her. "He's stubborn, arrogant, overbearing and spoiled. I wouldn't have him on a platter, if I were dying of hunger. I'd like to—"

She impatiently toweled her hair, finger combing it, and on impulse, placed the coronet on her head. She strolled out of the bathroom into the shadows of her bedroom.

Una's chest lay waiting on a doily, brass gleaming. While Fiona was brooding about Joel Palladin, she might as well wear Una's treasures. Fiona understood perfectly now, why Una had written so passionately about Tallchief, how his arrogance couldn't go unpunished, how she wanted revenge and yet she wanted the beauty of his kiss.

Fiona lifted the lid, sifted through the contents and chose a sky blue and white beaded necklace. She tied the leather thong behind her neck, drawing the triple-strand necklace close against her throat; she rummaged to find the heavy, barbaric, Celtic bracelet and slipped it on her wrist. The brass gleamed now since she'd earlier spent her anger polishing it. She touched the light doeskin shift that had belonged to Una, treasured and worn at the Tallchiefs' weddings. Blue beads depicting Tallchief Mountain warmed beneath her palm. Now the shift was hers, waiting for her to wear as a bride. "I don't need a bridal tepee. But if I had one, Joel Palladin wouldn't be sharing it. I'd want a nice, sweet man."

Taking care, Fiona lifted the flower coronet from her hair and eased the soft doeskin shift over her, the fringes sliding enticingly along her arms and legs. The coronet completed the picture of a bride as Fiona folded her arms in front of her and frowned. She studied herself in the mirror. She would wallow in her roses and plan how to demolish Joel—

Joel Palladin's face loomed behind her, his image and hers trapped in the shadows of the mirror, ferns quivering between them.

"You!" She pivoted to him, heart leaping and fringes flying.

"It took you long enough to get here," he said. "I don't want you running over dangerous mountain trails at night again, dear heart. See that you don't." Joel rose out of the chair in the shadowed corner of the room, walking slowly to her. He reminded her of a warrior—broad-shouldered, grimly determined—carefully picking his way through a delicate potted jungle of fuchsia flowers and ferns. "Are you done crashing through the place, muttering to yourself about how despicable I am and how you wouldn't have me on a platter if you were dying of hunger?" he asked, his voice too soft and mild.

"The reckoning" Una had called it. A wild pleasure skittered over Fiona's skin. The hunter had come calling for her. She saw it in the angle of his head, the muscle contracting and releasing in his jaw and the dark, impatient narrowing of his eyes.

"I don't like rules about what I do, or don't do," she stated carefully. "I'm used to running at night, Palladin. I do what I want."

This was her reckoning, this night with Joel, and she would have him. She refused to move, locking her feet to the carpet as the shadows and the heat of Joel's body swirled around her. She knew how to stand and fight and she would, bracing herself. He'd showered, dressed in a black sweater and jeans, his hair damp and gleaming. The scent of soap and male caught her.

"Get out," she ordered in a tone she hoped was cool and in control. The order was automatic, a thrust sent to test him. She'd ordered other men from her; if he left now, she would have to rethink, recircle Joel and waylay him on her terms, not his. "You have no right to be here."

"I think I do. You're furious, Fiona, and trembling, all decked out in your Scots and Tallchief dowry. I wonder why?" Joel's finger strolled down her cheek, his gaze locked with hers. "It suits you...no other woman could wear this outfit and still look breathtaking...the wild, high pride, savage mix of Scots and Sioux, of seer and shaman magic, Una's gray eyes and Tallchief's darker skin, his black glossy hair."

His fingertip rested in the hollow of her throat, her pulse racing against the light touch. "Do you know how enticing, enchanting you are, Princess? How your eyes flash like steel or darken into night smoke when you toss out a challenge? How you soften and flow in my hands like warm, living silk?"

His fingertip lifted her chin, his gaze shadowed and intent, roaming her face, seeing too much.

"What do you want?" she asked, her heart leaping higher, gearing into overdrive.

His fingers feathered through her cropped hair. "For two years I've dreamed about that shining black silk swirling around you from the time you stalked into my office. Then, it almost touched your waist," he remarked mildly, his hands coming up to spear through her hair, drawing her mouth close to his.

Could she give him her body and not her heart?

Then Joel lifted her against his chest. His first kiss was so light, she held his head, urging his mouth to hers, slanting it, fusing them with the hunger burning her. "You know that I can't resist a good challenge," she whispered.

"Sweetheart, the novelty of being pursued by you is fascinating," Joel returned, easing down into the chair with her on his lap.

She leaned back on those shoulders that were meant for cradling her head. As he settled her closer against him, she looked up at him and placed her palm over his heart. She needed the solid beat to steady her leaping fears. With her hand, she traced the angle of his shoulder, the taut muscle in his upper arm. This would be her first time with a lover, sharing herself. She feared the doors this reckoning would open, revealing her tenderness for Joel Palladin. She wouldn't let him close her away in that quick, hard way of his, not now.

His hand opened on her stomach, smoothing it, and Fiona tensed, unused to caresses. "I'm not your daughter, nor your sister. Admit it, Palladin. You're a cuddler."

"What if I am?" he asked with a growling edge that told her she'd pinned the truth. Joel liked sheltering his edges, but his desire licked at her like a flame, unbidden and bold.

Fiona placed her hand over his, and the tremor sweeping through him pleased her. He'd come for her, to hold her close and nuzzle her cheek with his. She'd chosen a sensual man, a toucher, and one who enjoyed women. Watching him, she slowly lifted his hand to her doeskin-covered breast.

"Is this an experiment?" Joel shot at her harshly, even though his palm cupped her, his thumb lightly caressing the tip of her breast.

"This is a seduction. Tonight you are mine, Joel Palladin," she whispered, giving way to the song moving within her. Her hum crossed her lips in a soft melody, and Joel's body tensed as she began to sing "Greensleeves."

He angled his head away from her hand, from the exploration of fingertips and palm fitted along his jaw. She sang to him, wooing him in an old-fashioned way that seemed perfect, this strange, tender, wary man with emerald eyes and dark skin heating, burning to her touch. Yet his heart raced beneath her breast, his hands firm and trembling upon her body.

She smoothed the lines on his forehead, circled his ear and nibbled on it in passing. His heartbeat pounded against her lips when she brushed them over his throat and on to the cleft in his chin.

When she had finished singing, Joel sat very still beneath her, trembling once as though held by an invisible bond. His body was hard; she recognized the desire she had raised in him, tempting his control. Oh, she would have no controlled man as her lover, but one that gave her the truth of his desire. His lips barely moved as she nibbled them. "I could hurt you, Fiona. I—"

"You won't. I've chosen you as my lover, Joel Palladin. You'll take no more of me than I would give." She eased from his lap and stood in the square of moonlight coming from the window as he rose to his feet, towering over her.

Amid her ferns, lacy curtains, doilies, hand-fashioned quilts and feminine clutter, Joel's size and angular body looked huge, alien and terrifying.

Fear skittered through her, causing her hands to tremble as she lifted the shift over her head. She folded it as gently as Una must have, so long ago, and turned slowly to Joel. She stood very straight, shy of him and of herself, as his gaze strolled down her body, touching, heating, lingering. "Undress," she whispered, uncertain of the hows and the whys and the mystery that he would give her.

Joel moved too slowly, easing away his sweater and tossing it to the floor. His chest fascinated her, all angular and gleaming and lightly dusted with hair. His worn boots were kicked aside, and then he stepped free of his jeans to reveal silk shorts. She couldn't resist placing the flower coronet on his head, for she would have her mark upon him when the reckoning came.

"Shy?" she challenged him, hungry for him as she moved to her bed. She should leave him now, be sensible and keep herself safe. If he removed the braided wreath, her claim to him, the magic would fly away into the moonlight—

"There is something you should know, Princess. My parents weren't married when I was born. Mamie didn't know anything about her bastard grandson until my mother showed up on her doorstep with a year-and-a-half-old child. She made her playboy son marry my mother. He resented it and blamed me." The words came curling bitterly out of him, born by pain. Fiona knew instinctively that he'd never told anyone. She wanted to hold him and whisper comfort, but Joel looked too proud, as she would have been.

"If you think that bit of irrelevant news can save you from my clutches, you're mistaken," she whispered unevenly, trying to keep a light note to ease his darkness.

"Get in the bed," he murmured pleasantly, standing on the other side, his body outlined by silvery moonlight.

She could order him away; he'd just handed her an excuse. She could leave. She could sleep by his side and listen to him breathe as she had at the ranch. She could hold Joel close and safe and warm. She could take what ran strong and heated between them. *This was her reckoning....*

Fiona lifted the old quilt and slid beneath it, smoothing it with her hands as she settled back to watch Joel. All angles and corded muscles and gleaming moonlit skin, Joel's body was rigid, his hands curled into fists.

"I won't hurt you," she said, patting the empty place beside her. "Come to Fiona."

"You look like a bride." The words seemed torn from him, his deep murmur raw and uneven.

"Come to bed. Come hold me, Joel," she whispered, aching for him. She held the bouquet of roses to him, a small gift to show him that she treasured the coming reckoning.

For a time, he studied the red petals, dusting his fingers across the delicate edges. She knew she would remember his expression forever—an almost shy, boyish pleasure. He almost glows, she thought, and she knew she had captured some small endearing part of him to hold close in later years.

He came to her slowly, the small bed dipping with his weight, the air cooling as he lifted the covers to slide beside her and study the length of her body. His fingertip touched her breast, and she almost cried out with the pleasure jolting through her. His mouth brushed hers, slanted, fused and dived into her heat.

"Fiona," he whispered urgently against her throat, his kisses flowing lower, heating, until his mouth covered her breast. She hadn't expected the exquisite pleasure as he suckled her, the gentle sensual tugging, drawing from her, giving her an intimate, moist warmth that his fingers found and stroked.

The flick of his tongue caught her unaware, tipping her hunger. She couldn't wait, hunger storming through her, her hands locking to his head, drawing him up to kiss her. She opened her eyes for a moment when he lifted his head; he was what she wanted, all angles and desire for her, heat melding his body to hers. Her hands skimmed down his sides, tracing the hard length of his body, from wide shoulders to narrow waist, to the tight backside she adored.

He was who she wanted, she thought, hurrying through her emotions because she knew that soon she would not be able to think. She had chosen him as her first lover.

Joel eased himself over her, never breaking the kiss that began lightly and stepped into a fiery hunger. *This is what I want,* Fiona thought as his body lay heavy and intimate upon hers. *He's wearing my mark, the braided flowers serving as a temporary wedding band...because she'd just discovered that she couldn't dismiss tradition, not with Joel.* "You're a lovely man, Joel Palladin, but if you don't have me soon, I'll die," she whispered before biting his lip.

"How would you know?" he asked, humor in his deep, uneven voice.

"Don't let me frighten you from your task, Palladin," she whispered just as raggedly, breathing hard as his hands went beneath her, cupping her bottom and lifting her higher.

He came into her slowly, like smooth, hot steel seeking a proper sheath, a warm home to nestle and love. She tensed, pain she hadn't expected shafting through her the moment he touched the barrier. Joel shuddered, one hand lifting to stroke back her damp hair, his thumb sliding across her lips. It was then that she saw his dragon, flexing in the moonlight, and reached out to claim his arm.

"You're mine," she whispered, arching for his kiss, meeting his tongue with hers, her fingertips digging into his shoulders, for he was not leaving her now.

Joel's body shuddered as she arched against him, bringing him deeper. While Fiona's body adjusted to the gentle invasion, she studied his expression as he stilled for a moment and shared her pillow. Desire warred with another fierce emotion she did not understand. To soothe him, she kissed him lightly. "There. That wasn't so bad, was it?"

The smile that came slowly curling to his lips pleased her more than roses. Reaching toward the bouquet on the bedside table, she took three roses. She tore the petals free and let them fall upon his head, spilling onto her. She would give him roses or wildflowers, bluebells from the meadows on Tallchief Mountain. She would hold him close and play with him until he gave her that boyish grin, the one he hid so well.

"You're full of yourself, Tallchief," Joel noted unevenly, pleasantly.

"Rather, you're providing the full part," she whispered back, shy with him now, this man who shared her body, her very heartbeat, whose tender expression had caused her tears, not the pain. She buried her hot cheeks in the safe cove of his shoulder and throat. "Yes, I've got tears in my eyes, and don't let them terrify you. They are because this is so lovely."

"It is...lovely." His teeth nibbled gently on her shoulder, then kissed it. "Better?"

"Much better." Fiona arched up to him, snaring him with her arms and dragging him close to her, chest to breast, stomach to stomach, hips and thighs locked perfectly, completely. She luxuriated in the feel of his body, angular and rough, against her own, in the strength surrounding her, caressing her, in the beautiful mouth claiming hers and tasting of her own hunger.

She hadn't expected the pounding of her desire, the burst of pleasure that circled her body, clenching it fiercely, driving it out of her control. She hadn't expected the fiery circles to come flashing behind her lids, nor the vision of a dragon, tamed and nestling in mountain wildflowers, nor her body flying into sunshine. The sensual impact jarred her and tossed her upon a warm, mellow, golden cloud, too filled with pleasure to move. When she managed to lift her lids, Joel was smiling tenderly down at her. "Having fun?"

She should have been angry because he appeared in control, while she had as much control as melting butter. But in her warm fuzzy cloud, anger wasn't possible. Joel looked too appealing and unexplored. Flexing intimate muscles she had just discovered, Fiona caught him deeper and enjoyed his quick confusion and delight. "You can come with me, this time, Palladin," she whispered, locking herself fiercely to him.

This time the fury hit her, Joel's body thundering over hers, their tempo matching beat for beat, and suddenly the riveting pleasure coursed into another tempo, a faster stream bearing them upward, higher, and in that heartbeat, Fiona felt absolute freedom, like an arrow shooting into the sunlight and falling gently into a field of wildflowers—

Joel's body tensed, and another fierce hot wave shot over Fiona as he shuddered, pouring himself into her.

His head lowered gently to her breast, his skin hot and flushed, his mouth brushing against her skin. Fiona lay quietly beneath his weight, his racing heart slowing upon her softness, his body lax and warm and draped pleasantly over hers. She nuzzled his hair, kissing it, stroking his shoulders and his back, pleased that he'd exposed his softer emotions to her, his vulnerability. He wasn't the meticulously clad executive now shielded by ice and power; rather he was rumpled and comfortable and sexy, yet arrogant enough to challenge her.

Joel's large hand prowled over her breasts, caressing them slowly, gently, as if treasuring her. Slowly his fingers smoothed her side, curled around the indentation of her waist, traced her hip and smoothed her thigh.

Fiona smiled softly into his hair. Whatever demons drove Joel Palladin, he was hers to protect now. She nestled beneath him, the wild need to possess him temporarily sated.

She inhaled slowly, drifting into sleep. She had claimed Joel Palladin, taken him as a lover, and now the game was on.

She dozed and awoke to the heat of his mouth on her breasts, tugging, nibbling, causing the cords to ignite within her, stirring her womb, her intimate warmth flowing—then he was sliding into her, filling her, taking her breath into his mouth and demanding that she meet him there in the fiery circle where all began and all ended. This time she gave him everything, the wildness within her, the savage need to claim him, the heat and the storms that sprang from deep inside her.

Aye and blast, she thought as the storm slammed into her, tightening her body, causing her to cry out then bite his shoulder to quiet the storms within her. She reached to hold his arm, the dragon upon it, claiming him once more. She unfurled gloriously, melting beneath him. She had chosen a wild lover, one with a warm cherishing mouth and tender hands; it would be a good match—if not love.

She opened her eyes to see Joel over her, his expression tender, knowing. "That wasn't fair," she said. "You didn't give me a warning."

He eased to one side, drawing her up close to him as he covered her bare shoulder with the quilt. "No, and I don't intend to in the future. All rules are off, Tallchief. You're too enticing. All those little purrs at the back of your throat, your sharp teeth nibbling on me and your fingers locked to my backside as if you crave me more than—ouch!"

He rubbed his injured chest and the hair she had just lightly tugged. Fiona shivered, startled by her embarrassment, her shyness of him. He chuckled when she burrowed close, holding him tightly, for he wasn't getting away from her just yet.

Fiona knew her smile was smug.

She'd entered the circle to claim her dragon.

Seven

Five o'clock the next morning came too soon for Fiona, the telephone ringing shrilly beside her bed. Because Joel's sizable body lay between her and the telephone, she decided to let the answering machine respond. She wallowed in the scents of crushed rose petals, the quick shower she had taken and the freshly bathed male, sleeping deeply at her side. Hours earlier, her shower had been brief, a private reckoning that her body had changed. Joel must have taken his recently, his hair was still damp. The flower coronet had been replaced, as though Joel treasured his trophy.

She arched and stretched luxuriously, her muscles aching pleasantly and her body floating in a warm, fuzzy and sated cloud. She snuggled closer to the sleeping man in her bed, wrapping her arm around Joel's lean waist. Since her leg was already between his, she stroked his calf with her sole, enjoying the textures of hard muscles covered by hair-roughened skin. She stroked his flat stomach and circled the indentation of his naval, causing him to moan lightly and suck in his breath. With his hair rumpled, the flower coronet askew, the dark stubble of a new beard showing on his jaw and his bare shoulder beneath her cheek, he did not resemble Palladin's immaculate, cool and controlled Iron Man. Fiona scooped up a handful of petals and let them fall onto his face. She'd done a good job of removing that image, Fiona decided smugly, placing a rose petal on the smile on his lips.

Before the second ring, he blew away the rose petal she had just placed upon his nose. He leaped from sleep into reality with jarring speed, ripping away the quilt impatiently and sitting up as he grabbed the phone. "Palladin here. What's up?"

Fascinated by her lover, who was now all business, Fiona tugged the quilt higher over her bare, sensitive breasts and studied Joel's rippling back, the dim, predawn light causing it to gleam. The red marks caused by her nails shocked her; she hadn't known she'd held him so fiercely. Then she remembered her high, wild cry, her body clasped desperately to the hard flex of his as they plunged— Because she needed to keep their reckoning warm and flowing, as dawn and reality approached, she kissed the marks, smoothing them with her fingertips; Joel tensed as he listened.

"Yes, I'm glad Rafe thought of this number. No, it's fine." He glanced over his shoulder at her and frowned as he spoke, "Uh-huh. Get Smythe on it. Have him working on deflecting the negative publicity and holding off the reporters. If the company was deficient in cleanliness before we purchased it, I didn't find it in the reports, and Rafe personally inspected the property— uh!" Joel reached behind him and captured Fiona's fingers, which had been walking slowly over his back.

He took her wrist as she curled closer to adjust the coronet of flowers. "The lab should be able to trace—"

Joel glanced down at Fiona's inner wrist. He frowned and smoothed the bruises with his thumb. "Palladin has always had a good team. When Mamie wakes up, make certain she knows. Let her have her morning coffee first. You can handle it, Doug. I trust you."

He clicked on the bedside lamp and lifted Fiona's arm to the light, studying it as he listened. His hand ran lightly across a pattern of bruises, matching them to his fingers. "Mamie caught Cody, did she? She's had plenty of experience with boys who want to run away from home. Tell my son that I'm looking forward to seeing him, will you? I know…he's not exactly happy with me for jerking him away from his friends in Denver. I've been getting threatening faxes from someone who thinks I don't belong on an isolated ranch…too bad Mamie's personal fax number is at the top of the paper and Cody's misspelling is pretty distinctive.''

Before he shielded his expression, turning his head from her, Fiona caught Joel's pain and the shadows leaping upon him, devouring him. She had to protect him, keep him tethered close to her. She eased her arms around him from the back and placed her chin in the hollow of his throat. She toyed with the damp curls at his nape and blew in his ear.

Joel eased away from her, dismissing her as he continued his conversation, a methodical checklist of what Doug must do to stave off unwanted publicity. ''Until Palladin, Inc. can get a grasp of the damage. If you need to, put Mamie out in front of the cameras. She can charm the newspapers and buy time, without giving them the time of day.''

Fiona smiled against Joel's back and kissed it. He liked his life private, his emotions firmly locked around him. Too bad, she was in the same bed.

Joel glanced back at Fiona, just when she was studying his firm backside cushioned in rose petals. She was just on the verge of patting his backside and placing her aching breasts against the smooth expanse of his back. Fiona jerked up the covers, feeling far too fragile and uncertain. He ran the back of his hand across her hot cheek as he dealt with business. Fiona squirmed away as his fingertip slid under the beaded thong to trace the tender patches on her throat where his rougher skin had abraded her own.

After her shower—a private time to recover from the shattering pleasure she hadn't expected—she'd replaced the leather beaded necklace; she'd noted the scrape marks and the slight bruises on her throat. She'd accepted them, the honest aftermath of Joel's passion. He had been more than gentle, yet she'd been too eager, too fierce in her needs, the novelty of his heat and desire igniting her own.

Joel gently tugged down the blanket, and she watched his expression harden, his eyes darkening, chilling, as he found other scrapes on her breasts. A muscle contracted beneath the dark skin on his upper cheek, a vein throbbed heavily in his temple. He jerked the flower coronet from his head, tossing it aside as though it disgusted him.

With it went the tenderness she had been feeling for him; Fiona jerked the covers up to her breasts and locked them in place with her arms.

Fiona set her jaw, glaring at him. He didn't deserve tenderness or the flowers. This was the morning after her claiming of him. The least he could do was to serve her one of those marvelous, delicious, tempting, heated kisses. She'd expected another... pleasure from Joel. It was the least he could do after giving her so much delight earlier. Her greed for Joel had surprised her. She didn't feel like shooing him from her bed, but rather she'd prefer to have—

"I'll run your bath," he said as smoothly as ordering a perfectly cooked steak or planning a conference room. Or maybe the cool tone came from experience with other women. Fiona tensed, scrambling for reason. Of course Joel had had other liaisons; she expected that. But they weren't Fiona Tallchief.

"I've had a shower." She saw no reason to spare him; she'd expected a beautiful morning after, and now Joel was glaring at her, his defenses up. Fiona shivered; she felt like crying and she wouldn't give him one tear. *Weren't lovers supposed to say thank-you, that was lovely, et cetera, et cetera?* "Shouldn't you be going?" she asked curtly, furious with herself for expecting— What? Romance? Commitment? Tenderness?

"You're in a nasty mood," Joel noted, giving her nothing of rose petals and kisses and—

She inhaled, preparing to tell him just where to leap and what to stuff. The telephone rang again, and when she jerked it to her ear, Birk snapped, "Baby sister, just wait until Duncan hears about this— Palladin's car has been parked in the back alley of your shop since last night. Calum just called. He was out on the porch retrieving a present he'd hidden for Talia and wearing nothing but his goose bumps when the sheriff's loudspeaker caught him. The sheriff was impressed by the tenor tapes lying on Palladin's car seat. The sheriff broadcast that to Calum, and now the whole town knows."

"I'll handle this, Birk. Tell the Black Knights to back off. Now, you know I love you all, but you're not rescuing Palladin from me. I intend to teach him a lesson."

While she listened to Birk, a former ladies' man, mutter and worry over his baby sister, Fiona studied Joel, who was scowling fiercely at her, a deep wave crossing his forehead. He looked perfectly exciting—wary, stubborn, rumpled and ready for her platter.

"Life is good," she stated with a grin, excitement surging through her as she firmly replaced the receiver. "Things were getting pretty boring. Are you frightened, Palladin? Can you keep up?"

Joel took a deep breath, the vein in his temple pulsing as he stared at her lips, which she had just tested with her tongue. "I've got to get out of here," he muttered, looking for his shorts.

"Why?" she asked, suddenly afraid, all her courage and excitement pooling at her feet. "Wasn't I...wasn't this...?"

"You just don't get it, do you?" he shot at her. "I haven't had that much experience, but I've always been in control, and this time I wasn't. I could have hurt you. Those bruises on your wrist—" He looked pale, ill and disgusted as he took her wrists in both hands to study the two slight marks. "I *did* hurt you."

He hadn't had that much experience. Fiona gloried in the admission.

He glanced down at the bloodstain on her sheets and turned paler. He pushed her wrists away and looked down at his hands. spreading them, as though bad memories had glued themselves to his fingers and would not be shaken away. "He hurt my mother. I was only three or four, but I remember. He hurt Rafe and Nick, and there was nothing I could do to stop him. I never thought I would— I am his son—"

Frightened by this insight into Joel's horrible past, and desperate to pry him from it, Fiona raised her hands to frame his face. "Joel, please do not be disappointed, but I'm not delicate. What happened last night between us was honest, passionate and real.

It was exactly what I wanted. I took you, and you responded. I take responsibility for my needs. End of story.''

He kissed her wrists, one by one lingering over the bruises in an apology so earnest and humble that it frightened her. She tried to give him an easy way to leave her; she would not have him obligated to her. "This has nothing to do with your father or any legacy you may think you've inherited from him—which you haven't. I have excellent judgment in the company I keep, Joel. My instincts have never failed me. I told you that I am a physical woman, wanting a suitable partner. You fitted the bill. We had a passionate night, Joel Palladin, nothing more. Don't make too much of it. Those hours are behind us, and now we can go on with our lives—''

Joel's head lifted abruptly, his green eyes flashing, raking her. His smile came slowly, coldly, distant. "Now that we've faced our demons, so to speak? Satisfied our sexual attraction? We can call it quits? Playtime is finished. Is that how you see it?" he shot rapid-fire at her, reminding her of his attorney background.

She shivered. In her lifetime only a handful of men, including her brothers, had had as much impact as Joel, and none of them had caused the hair on her nape to be raised. He looked like a medieval knight, wrapped in his cape and ready to draw his sword.

"It was a reckoning. I knew it would happen, so did you—'' She wouldn't ask him to stay. How could he look so cold and furious when she wanted his arms around her, holding her close?

Joel stared at her for a long, breathless moment. Then he placed his open hand on her forehead and gently pushed her back onto the bed. She scrambled under the quilt and pulled it higher, as she watched him dress. "Why are you so angry?" she asked as he grabbed the flower coronet on his way out.

With his hand on her bedroom door, Joel turned slowly to her. While Minnie purred and twined around his legs, he looked at Fiona so long that she found herself blushing furiously, the covers up to her chin. She hated blushing and feeling fragile; she'd given him a portion of herself, an insight into her needs, and he knew her at a primitive level that frightened her. They both knew that Fiona's acceptance of his body was significant, because she had been meticulous about her life, waiting to choose a lover who was unique. Joel knew he was that lover; he knew that she wouldn't leap from him into another man's arms. He knew their first lovemaking had delighted her and that there was a bond brewing between them.

He knew too much. A rose petal came tumbling from the top of her hair, down to her nose, and she blew it away, glaring at him. She would have to be very careful with Joel, an analytical, methodical man, who understood her on a level she hadn't explored. He could be dangerous to her. Fiona did not want to be dissected, formulized and nudged into the traditional woman that would be Joel's ideal.

They both knew he wasn't what she wanted, a man who liked rules and structure. Fiona foraged for defense and words to toss at him. "I do not like how you line up your tools next to the motor you are repairing," she said very properly. "I notice that all the handles are parallel and rest on an imaginary straight line. You could never make exciting flower arrangements. You are not impulsive."

Joel's gaze narrowed, claiming her, cruising her bare shoulders over the blanket. She tugged it higher.

"But I am very thorough and I like to see my projects through," he drawled, reminding her of their earth-shattering lovemaking. "That's more like it. I like it when you blush, Princess," he said with another tight, grim smile as if he'd accomplished what he wanted. Then he quietly closed the door behind him.

The quiet click of the latch echoed loudly, as though Joel Palladin had had what he wanted from her and was not returning.

Fiona swallowed, her throat tight with emotion; she had taken what she wanted, an equal affair.

Joel cruised his sports car up Duncan Tallchief's driveway and parked in front of the house. He cut the motor, stepped free of the car and scanned the house where Fiona had lived as a child. On the last October Sunday, Tallchief Mountain jutted from the Rockies, looking like a cold fortress. Fiona's Morning Star was in the corral and a herd of Tallchief cattle grazed in the field.

Joel walked around the Corvette. On the afternoon after claiming Fiona, his first virgin, he was still rocked by that first tight penetration and Fiona's dismissal of commitment this morning. Her clinical dissection of their lovemaking had upset him. A man accustomed to dealing with Palladin's intricate corporate structure and his clinically tailored life, Joel hadn't expected his unsteady emotions.

His experience in delicate, bruised emotions with a woman who had selected him, left him uneasy. He felt as if Fiona, the physical woman, had rummaged through the males on the shopping shelf and had chosen him. While it was a compliment—in one way— Joel wasn't certain it suited him.

For hours Palladin's top corporate attorney had been sighing over Fiona's braided, wilted, flower headpiece, twirling it around his fingers and thinking of how Fiona had looked, simmering beneath him, spilling rose petals over his head. Later her comment about his inability to make artistic flower arrangements had wounded him. He liked his tools in a line and ready for his hand; all the handles should rest equally spaced and in a straight line.

For a concession, he mentally angled his smallest prized screwdriver, the one with the magnetic tip, tilting it a little to the right.

Thirty-seven was a fine time to discover that he was a traditional man and that he was a romantic, that he needed hugs and kisses the morning after she had her way with him, despite his control. Fiona's "fine, we've had sex, we're done" attitude grated. He'd dreamed of cooking breakfast, serving it to her with a rose and himself and trying words that he'd never said before, dreams he'd never realized.

Dreams weren't for him; however, romance if dissected and carefully reconstructed along a model line, would equate to fine-tuning the small motors he loved so much. He knew he could be romantic once he ingested, digested and decided what women—one woman in particular—wanted. The magazine racks were full of information. First, women usually liked appropriate presents. She liked lacy lingerie—Joel grinned, sliding into the thought of Fiona's long, lean sexy body hugged by lace. Joel scanned the Tallchief pastures leading into the pines that would become wild forests. But then, rebels were never easy to catch, and Fiona did not like rules or ties.

Joel glanced up to Tallchief Mountain where he'd first seen Fiona hurling herself toward him and yelling threats. Her parents lay behind her in the meadow; his father the reason for her grief. One day he would have to visit them. Joel ran his hand across his jaw and prayed that Fiona did not hold their deaths against him or his family. In her circumstance, he didn't know if he could excuse the damage.

He walked around the cats sprawled on the warm, sunlit sidewalk and glanced at the three huge dogs lying on the front porch. Their unwelcoming, alert expressions reminded him of the Tallchief brothers.

Sybil's invitation to the Tallchiefs' Sunday dinner was perfect for establishing base rules. Joel carefully extracted the flower wreath from his pocket and placed it on his head. Though frayed and wilting, it represented Fiona's claiming of him. He hadn't been claimed before, and the novelty pleased him. Joel grinned to himself, suddenly feeling boyish and excited about his first girl. He wasn't finished with Fiona; he would physically control his passion for her—taking care to shave before coming close to her fine skin, and—Joel shuddered. There would be no more bruising. The next time Fiona was in his bed—Joel inhaled abruptly. He would be very careful with her next time.

Though he was wearing his favorite, battered leather jacket, Joel had dressed carefully. He bent to dust his Italian loafers with a handkerchief, glanced at his expensive hand-knit sweater and raised his hand to the big *T* door knocker. Poised, he listened intently to the happy ruckus inside—a child giggled wildly, a woman worried if the turkey was moist, another if they would have enough dressing, and deeper tones of men coursed through a baby's furious demands. This was what Joel wanted for Cody, a warm home and a family.

Joel inhaled the crisp mountain air, filled with the scent of pine. "I will try, son."

Dressed in her kilt and plaid, Elspeth swept out to the porch, looped her arm through his and tugged him into the huge living room. She helped him remove his jacket and hung it in the closet.

The weaver of the family, Elspeth said, "Your sweater is a lovely shade of emerald green. It matches your eyes. We're glad you came."

Shocking him, Elspeth had been the first woman to note the color of his eyes. He wondered sullenly if Fiona had noticed. "I would have brought flowers, but the local florist—"

Elspeth winked at him. "The local florist doesn't know you're coming. She can get nasty, but I think you can handle her."

A child crawled across Joel's Italian loafer, studied it for a moment and then sank down to teethe upon it. At the same time a toddler lurched from Talia's lap, took four steps and grabbed Joel's Armani slacks with both sticky fists.

Also dressed in their Tallchief kilts and plaids and standing in front of the fireplace, the brothers stared at him, as though he deserved tar and feathers. The teething child pulled herself upon his other pant leg. Joel, fearing to move and hurt a child, stood absolutely still. Sybil hurried by, carrying a huge bowl of salad on her way to the long dinner table. "I am so irritated by Marcella Portway. She just called. I'm a professional genealogist, Joel, and I hunt family treasures—oh, you know that, don't you? You were very good to acquire Una's chest before me. Anyway, Marcella Portway is determined that she's related to Spanish royalty. If she is, I can't find it." She glanced at the children latched on to Joel's slacks. "I hope you like children," she added.

Joel looked down the distance to the black-haired, gray-eyed girls and imagined Fiona as a child…as a woman carrying his child. He blinked, feeling off-balance. This, he excused, was because he'd awakened feeling like a groom. In his current reasoning, groom led to family man, Fiona in his arms all night and babies. He felt himself go light-headed, a rarity for Palladin's Iron Man.

He hadn't expected the tender emotions swirling around him, the buffeting need to become a family man. He hadn't been invited to Cody's birth and actually knew little about his son. After Cody's conception, Joel had learned that his ex-wife had wanted a child to ensure her hold at Palladin, Inc. He wanted Cody to have this family's warmth, with brothers and sisters tucked around him. Joel wanted to be…"Pa."

There were steps preceding lover, groom and pa. Fiona, rebel that she was, had skipped wooing Joel. He felt deprived and fragile.

Damn. Add romance to his personal fragile list, Joel decided, because he wanted to romance Fiona in a traditional way.

He noted the dining room table's glorious, wild arrangement of flowers and greenery, which reminded him of Fiona, color splashing, spilling everywhere. Joel concentrated on the design and frowned, searching for the theme, the angles, the motif. It eluded him. *With effort, he could be impulsive, despite Fiona's sterile opinion of him.*

Joel studied the Tallchiefs' babies and children. To his knowledge he wasn't sterile, and he'd been impulsive enough not to use his newly purchased supply of protection. The odds of Fiona conceiving on their first night were not high, yet possible—he heard his wistful sigh and stifled it. In his life he dealt with the reality of necessities, not dreams. A family and children would be too much to ask.

Emily, Sybil's seventeen-year-old daughter, was placing the silver on woven napkins. "He's got the look," she noted wisely.

"Oh, no, he hasn't," Calum, Duncan and Birk stated at the same time, glaring at Joel.

"Not with our baby sister," Calum added firmly.

"She's always loved a good battle. Look at him. Though he doesn't look like it now with the girls around him, I'll bet Fiona won't be bored. Apparently, from childhood, she's terrorized her share of males. He looks like he could keep up," Talia stated with a grin.

"Well, there is Una's dragon and chest legend, you know," Elspeth noted cheerfully.

"That's right. There is that," Joel added smugly, his spirits lifting from the delicate-fragile zone. He reached down to pluck up a child in each arm. Unaccustomed to babies, Joel stood very still, adjusting to them. They squirmed and cuddled to him, smelling of baby powder, laundry softener and innocence.

He returned a juicy kiss first to one and then to the other, just as Fiona came into the room in a swirl of her kilt and plaid, her face flushed and her eyes soft from playing with the baby in her arms. She stopped and stared at Joel while the two toddlers kissed his face, hugged him and pointed to the flowers on his head.

He would remember her forever, dressed in her frilled white shirt, with the Tallchief tartan plaid draped from shoulder to hip to the hem of her kilt. He hadn't had time to kiss those pretty knees, but he would, and all the rest of her he'd missed in their stormy, fast passion. Toe kissing was definitely added to his romantic list. Desire streaked through him again, skittered under his skin and hardened his body as Fiona's head went back. He was staring boldly and didn't care, fascinated by her.

This is my woman, he thought, a goddess of fire and storms and strength and tenderness. Yet she was very feminine, the arch of a brow, the sweep of her hand, the sway of her hips. My goddess, he added mentally. I'll never hurt her— He stiffened, remembering how he had held her tightly as they'd fought for release, remembering the slight bruises on her wrist and the blood on her sheet.

"What are you doing here?" Fiona demanded coldly, though a hot blush was slowly creeping up her cheeks. She eyed the flower wreath suspiciously.

Joel looked at her, his body tensing, muscle by muscle. Little kept him from going to her, sweeping her into his arms for a romantic Valentino kiss, and—on the other hand, he didn't enjoy feeling like the unwelcome remnants of last night's dinner. He was certain that when he got the hang of "romantic," he'd be more comfortable with Fiona.

"He's come for Sunday dinner, Fiona," Sybil said, patting him on the shoulder. Joel could have kissed her, his gratitude could even extend to baby-sitting.

"He doesn't need feeding. Don't fall for his helpless act. If you only knew how I cooked and cleaned—I even had plans to reform him and get him a job. Go home, Joel."

"You make a great housewife, Princess. I love it when you sing and mop." While she steamed, Joel fought the smile tugging at his lips.

"He'd look great in a kilt," Lacey, Birk's wife, noted with a grin as she took the toddlers.

Joel studied Fiona and knew he wanted more from life than corporate legalities, Italian and French brand names on his suits and shoes, and watches that cost fortunes. "I've never gone steady. You know, like in high school, when the girl wears the guy's ring," Joel admitted, and watched Fiona's expression go blank.

"You're a cool guy. Any guy who can give a girl an elephant is okay with me," Emily stated. "Let's eat."

Fiona frowned at him. "I'll want to talk with you privately. Please take off that ridiculous wreath."

"I'm a modern man, Princess. Instead of you wearing my ring, I'm wearing your wreath."

"I like his style," stated Alek, who had had to battle for Elspeth.

"Thanks." Joel glanced to the Tallchief brothers who were approaching, glowering at him.

"Oh, they're just bristling because they love Fiona and want to protect her...and dinner is waiting," Sybil said as she and the other wives grabbed their respective husbands. They herded their husbands to the table, plopped babies in their laps and hurried to adjust the high chairs that were placed around the table.

Talia indicated an empty place to Joel. "You'll have to sit by Fiona...unless she wants us to reorganize the whole table and all the high chairs."

Joel nodded. Talia deserved a free sample—bangle bracelets—from Palladin's newest jewelry acquisition. He noted Sybil's classic style and decided that pearl stud earrings would be suitable, a gold comb for Elspeth and a delicate ring for Lacey.

"You're staying here tonight, Fiona," Duncan ordered flatly while dipping potatoes onto his daughter's plate. He stared at Joel, a hands-off-my-baby-sister look.

After dinner Fiona folded her arms across her chest and studied the Tallchief males and Alek, all bent over, their heads beneath the hood of the sports car on the driveway and their kilts blowing in the wind. Joel was in the driver's seat, revving the engine, obviously wallowing in delight as he showed off his mechanical pet. He tossed a tool to Duncan, who grinned with delight and immediately dived under the hood. The sounds of revving followed, the males obviously delighted.

Fine-tuning an engine seemed to make friends of unlikely men. Raised with brothers and cars, she'd helped tune engines in her time, and she wasn't tuning Palladin's personal one.

"I could kick all my brothers' backsides. He's just seducing them, that's all." Throughout dinner Joel had ignored her.

He seemed little like the lover she'd held in her arms until five o'clock this morning. After he'd left, she'd gathered her bedding around her, keeping Joel's scents close; she'd hugged his pillow and hugged Una's chest close. She'd cried and muttered and slashed aside the bruised rose petals and then had picked up the old thread and the shuttle and begun tatting as she'd learned on her mother's lap. Her emotions caused her to flash through a foot of lace, full of mistakes at the beginning, then the design smoothing out as she decided her life was untouched by Joel—he simply did not matter.

Well, there was that matter of her heart tearing when he had closed the door.

Minnie, usually a playful cat swatting at thread, had sprawled upon the bed; she had studied Fiona with huge topaz eyes. Abe and George had made for the windowsill, sunning while Fiona had tatted furiously.

Then she remembered the sight of Joel holding the two Tallchief toddlers, the whimsical, battered wreath tilting rakishly on his head. It was heart stopping. Add his pleased grin and Joel could be—there was nothing so dangerous as this morning's lover looking like a potential father.

The Corvette's motor revved as Birk, an ex-race-car driver, leaned around the hood to speak to Joel.

Elspeth came beside Fiona, looping an arm around her shoulders. "It's clear to see that Joel isn't falling at your feet, despite wearing that wreath. When he finally did take it off, he was so careful with it, tucking it into his jacket pocket. You should have seen your expression when he announced that he was entering Maddy's Friday Night Tango and Talent Contest for charity. Amen Flats is buzzing. I just bet the casseroles and dinner invitations are arriving at his house right now. I wonder who will be his partner?''

''Aye. Women will fall all over him, and he'll win,'' Fiona muttered. She had experienced his technique, several of them in fact, and Joel was a champion when he set his mind to it.

She would not have her life constructed in neat little blocks.

''Mmm. There are rules to this game, Fiona,'' Elspeth murmured. ''He's out to claim you.''

Fiona snorted delicately. ''He's barely paid attention to me, and I'm not a woman to be claimed.''

Elspeth laughed. ''We'll see. Here they come, ready for more cherry pie and ice cream. They had better not wake the babies up from their naps. I like Joel Palladin, though he's as wary as you are. There is tenderness in him, and honor, too. Dad and Mom would have liked him. He's giving up everything to try to make a life for his son. He's a bit stiff around the edges, but in the midst of the Tallchiefs, I would expect that.''

''Joel is a very formal man. You should see his office. There isn't a paper clip out of place. He has rules for everything. His secretary said, 'You can't go in. Mr. Palladin's list of rules clearly says that—' Palladin's rules aren't for me. I won't have him put me on a list, setting up rules on male and female roles...his being the dominant, well-organized one, of course.''

Elspeth grinned. ''Oh, I think Joel is very adept at getting what he wants. He's probably willing to make adjustments.''

Fiona inhaled unevenly and straightened. Joel could entice her brothers with his toy and charm her family, but winning her over after leaving her this morning was another matter.

Joel came in the door, laughter on his lips and a sparkle in his eyes. Fiona's breath caught in her throat, her desire to kiss his beautiful mouth so strong she almost leaped upon him.

Joel stared at her; her heart seemed to kick up two beats, circled her chest and pattered merrily.

''Would you tango with someone else?'' she demanded in a whisper, and knew that if he held another woman close, a part of her would tear away. For there were rules attached, when a man looked at her that way.

Joel walked toward her, taking her hand. With the air of a

polished executive at a fancy corporate cocktail party, he smiled coolly, though the heat in his eyes jarred her into shivering. "We're going now. Fiona wants to discuss plants for my house, and we have to start practicing for the contest," he said smoothly.

While her brothers tried to find reasons why she shouldn't go with Joel, Fiona stared at him and blinked. He hadn't spoken to her, and now he was staking his claim as easily as ordering a second piece of pie.

"Wonderful," she tossed back, wanting privacy for cutting his arrogance in half.

"You can't just bring me to your house and toss me into your bed," Fiona whispered when Joel finally lifted his lips from hers.

Joel breathed rapidly, his face hot. "The gearshift was getting to me."

They were both breathing hard, tangled around each other. There was nothing smooth and polished about his heart racing against her breast, or his look strolling down her body—it reminded her of summer heat lying close and ready to erupt over a cool mountain meadow. Nor the hand smoothing her breast beneath her now-wrinkled, frilled shirt. His hand skimmed down her body, slid beneath her kilt and rose slowly, smoothly on her thigh. His boyish grin delighted her as he unfastened her brooch and tugged her Tallchief plaid away. He toyed with the buttons on her shirt. "Mmm. Let's see what's under all this—"

Fiona couldn't resist placing her hand upon the chest he'd just bared. "Joel..." she whispered, arching her body up to his, meeting his hungry kiss.

Hours later Fiona sat naked, bundled in a quilt with Joel, while they watched the firelight in his new freestanding woodstove. He tightened his arms around her, ran his lips along her cheek and nibbled at her earlobe, then he was silent, locking his thoughts from her, withdrawing to his private pain that lurked, never far away.

She held his hand, smoothing it, fitting the hard larger shape of his palm and fingers against her own. "Cody will adjust. Children do."

"I don't know if this is the right move, bringing him here."

Joel glanced at her, and seemed to withdraw within himself, as though he'd taken more pain than he could bear. "He's not happy with me. We have no relationship, and I come off feeling like a bully every time I try to help. I'm usually laying down rules, because he hasn't had that many. Patrice let him run wild. I was too wrapped up in my own life and thought he'd been getting better parental care. Her folks are great, and I thought she'd be better with him than me. That was a mistake I'll always regret. I yelled at him once, another something I regret," he added unevenly. The pain in Joel's tone caused Fiona to ache, for she knew that he was remembering how he'd been treated.

"You're nothing like your father, Joel."

"Aren't I?" The hard answer came back too weary, too old and ragged.

Fiona turned his head to hers and opened herself to him, giving Joel Palladin the tenderness he deserved. He drew away slowly, warily. "I'm not asking for sympathy or understanding. You like underdogs, Princess, and you are not getting my adoption papers. Whatever happens between us, it has to be honest. Agreed?"

Fiona moved over him, straddling him, and inhaled as she slowly took him into her body. The move was aggressive, experimental, and for Fiona, suited her needs. His hands cupped her bottom, caressing her. Joel's eyes were slits, and she knew that he had taken himself away momentarily, to enjoy the pleasure. "I'd say this is very honest. If you're looking for an adoption, try someone else."

Eight

"Joel is waiting out there on the street. It's the last week of October and the wind coming down from the Rockies cuts through to the bones. He must be freezing." Lacey smirked at Fiona over her cup of hot herbal tea.

Maddy, chewing on a lollipop instead of his usual cigar, hurried by with another pot of hot water. The Tuesday Ladies Night at Maddy's Hot Spot was rolling along, steeped in sodas, herbal tea and hot lemonade. "Smart Children Stories" were prohibited, and violators were removed after five marks on a blackboard. The Tallchief women sat at their table. Talia tapped her knee-high boots to a rock and roll tune. "I am really glad Maddy drapes sheets over the painted nudes on the wall," she said.

"Birk adores them. He says fully endowed women like that are an endangered species," Lacey said.

"Birk likes the small compact Venus types, and you know he's teasing, Lacey. I think Joel likes the long, lean ones," Sybil purred with a grin. "You're the last unmarried Tallchief, Fiona. From the look of Joel, I'd say he wants to change that."

Fiona flipped the price tag on the centerpiece of plastic roses.

"We're just practicing for the tango contest. We haven't even known each other for a month."

Or had they known each other forever? They had practiced everything, feeding upon each other, linking hands and bodies, fusing mouths...eager, hungry for each other. One look could set desire simmering.

Yet Joel kept a margin of control that caused her to want to shred him.

How was it possible for her to step into the delight and heat of their lovemaking, when he withheld a part of himself?

Buffeted by Joel's old-fashioned concerns that she be home in her own bed at night to prevent gossip, when she wanted to snuggle next to him, Fiona glanced outside. Joel leaned patiently against his small car, leather collar tugged high against the wind, shoulders hunched and long legs crossed at the ankle. Fiona scowled at him through the window. He was waiting to take her home, to protect her, and she'd had enough of older brothers restricting her freedom.

To finish the circle, an unlikely love of the battlemaiden will come calling, bearing his angry dragon on one arm and the chest to win her heart. Then the magic circle will be as true as their love....

Fiona flicked the price tag dangling from the plastic rose again. She wasn't certain she could adapt to Joel's analytical mind, the way he placed his tools at exactly the same distance apart and on that imaginary line. Lines and rules weren't for her. Nor was a man who had built his life on them....

She would have no rules between them, or in her life, not when it came to—what? Romance? Lovemaking? Intimacy? A relationship? Were their intimacy and her independence impossible?

How could Joel be so controlled when they made love? It was no easy matter for him, and she clung to that: Joel trembled, his expression stark and fierce, and yet he held his body in rein—

"Aye, and blast," she stated and surged to her feet. She impatiently smoothed her tight jeans. The storms hovering on Tallchief Mountain did not compare to her ragged emotions.

He'd given her an elephant and an insight into his painful past and fears. She was certain few women had seen that part of Joel;

therefore, he'd given her something uniquely private, placed it into her keeping.

"Aye and blast. I'm starting to think logically from *A* to *B*, just like him," she repeated, jerking down her thick wool jacket. She cared too much for him, and it went past the burning heat of their bodies, the excitement that arose from just looking at him. The give-and-take involved in a relationship with a man like Joel—analytical and methodical—could be...exciting, fulfilling...good. While he looked alone and deserted by fate now, Joel could look enchanting, boyish and playful. She intended to get the latter out of him. She intended to explore her own femininity, freeing the softness that lurked within her that she'd been too busy to explore. In one way Joel gave her freedom to explore her emotions, rather than shielding them. But everything had a price tag, she'd learned, and Joel had a big fat label on him that read, "Traditional." "He has real potential, but I am not adopting him."

The Tallchief women's eyebrows rose. "Joel Palladin?" they asked in unison.

"He's far too delicate with me, and we've got a tango to practice. He's given me an elephant, after all," Fiona muttered, moving out the door on her way to sort her Joel Palladin problems.

She crossed the street to him. The wind whipped his hair; he didn't move, legs crossed in front of him. She walked to one side of him, patted the car and walked to the other side, patting the hood and studying him. "I don't know about this, Joel," she began. "I'm used to my freedom."

She walked around him again, studying him up and down as she slapped the trunk. "I've always disliked the corporate male."

She returned to pat the hood on his prized car, drummed her fingers upon the shining metal as she considered the man who had entered her life. "What about your ex-wife? Why did you marry her?"

His beautiful mouth tightened. "It was logical. Her father was a friend of Mamie's. She came from a family that I liked...wonderful parents. I had worked with her father, admired him. Her mother was perfect. I thought I could have that family warmth, too. I wanted...more than work."

"She gave you a child. That is no small thing."

Joel looked off into the mountains, locking himself from her. Fiona understood; some things went too deep to share and Joel was a hoarder—

"I'm not proud of why Cody was conceived. Patrice wanted a child. I thought a child would enrich her life, give her what I couldn't seem to, and that she—" Joel inhaled sharply, his features tightening. "It seemed logical that a woman would want a baby, an extension of herself. I'd seen what babies do to women, making them happy and glowing. But Patrice resented Cody from her first bout with morning sickness, and when he arrived, looking so much like me— She reminded me that I was a bastard to her socialite standing and that I had nothing to give Cody," he added so softly, achingly that his words flew away on the wind.

Fiona nudged the expensive tire with her boot and continued to drum her fingers on the metal. She ached for him, but she had to know—"Is *logical* in our relationship?"

I won't settle for cold logic. I can't. Not P's and Q's all lined up in a straight line, waiting to be neatly arranged.

"It would be nice. But it isn't a requirement. I think we understand each other, and that is enough for me. For what it's worth, my ex-wife thought I was cold and unromantic."

Fiona stopped drumming her fingers and walked in front of him, placing her hands on her waist. Joel's lovemaking had been tender, deliciously romantic. "Don't lie to me. Not now."

He shrugged, giving her nothing; she could either believe him or not.

Oh, she'd get it out of him. Fiona pushed her finger against his chest. She scoffed at jealous women, and now jealousy filled her. "What about other women? You said you didn't have that much experience."

Joel lifted his head, glaring at her. "You go for the throat, don't you? I've been busy, Princess. If you're wanting a playboy, I don't fill the bill."

Fiona ran her hand up to his hair, letting it curl around her fingers as Joel angled his head, warily. He'd chosen her, this meticulous man, who managed his life according to clear thought, deduction, and—she stared at Joel, taking in his grim expression.

"Blast. You are monogamous. That's a trait of the traditional male, you know. That probably means you're committed to some sort of a relationship. My brothers are. What do you expect from me...commitment?"

"I expect you to give me what you want and nothing more. No false sense of rescuing me from myself...you're prone to jump into crusades, and I won't be one of them. I just discovered that traditional element myself, and I'm not that happy about it. You can drive," he said, tossing the car's keys to her.

"Aye and blast," she muttered, as he crossed in front of the car and slid into the passenger side. He'd given her something else precious to him, the steering wheel of his Corvette, and she'd been aching to drive it.

Fiona grasped the door handle and jerked it open. Sprawled in the open convertible, the wind whipping his hair, Joel placed his arm along the back of the seat. His look challenged her.

Fiona found herself grinning at him, excitement pounding at her. She'd take his challenge and— She adjusted the seat, started the motor, revved it and slid the car into first gear. Birk had taught her racing; he'd needed competition. "Where to?" she asked enjoying the cold air and the challenge of the man seated next to her.

He toyed with the hair feathering her nape. "Your choice, Princess."

"Blast. I had a feeling you'd say that." Because she had to, Fiona reached out to snag his jacket in her fist and draw his lips to hers for a fast, hard kiss.

Delighted, he laughed outright, and she grinned. "You're a cool one, Joel Palladin."

"Mmm. I confess. A structured planner. Analytical and organized," he agreed. "We'll see about the cool part."

"I think I'll have you first and while you're half dead, I'll have you again," she threatened with a grin and a saucily lifted eyebrow to let him know she was teasing.

Joel had to be handled very carefully when it came to teasing; those wary edges were never far from the surface.

"I'll try to survive." Joel placed his hand over her jeaned thigh. A woman not given to easy caresses and who had kept her body very private, Fiona glanced down at his hand. It seemed right, resting lightly upon her, and she placed her own over it.

She took him into the wild, windy, cold night, flying the small car over the road toward Tallchief Lake.

"You're good," Joel noted as she shifted smoothly, easing the car onto an unpaved side road. She liked the look of him at her side, sprawled in the small seat, hand resting on the outside of the car, the wind whipping at his hair.

She shifted again, taking care to ease over the rocks and bumps. "We should have stopped for my Jeep. It's a sad thing on the outside, but it's dependable and runs like a top. I tuned it myself," she tossed at him, as a big buck ran in front of the headlights.

When Joel glanced at her, surprised, she smirked. "I've always been good with motors. I seem to know where to touch them and what to tinker with."

The taut, desperate desire in Joel's expression delighted her. "Oh, hell," he murmured unevenly, as if he'd just sunk an inch lower in quicksand.

A half hour later Joel shuddered over her, his hot face tucked into the cove of her throat and shoulder. Fiona gathered him closer, keeping him near, when their passion was spent. Moonlight slipped through the pine boughs overhead, then clouds whisked across the sky, causing the night to go black and intimate and safe.

They'd made hot, fast love, his leather jacket beneath them and the wild cold night wrapped around them.

She'd given him more each time they'd touched, opening herself to the pleasure and the beauty.

This was what she loved, held safe in his arms, intimacy flowing like warm wine over them. She hadn't expected the softness within her, the need to gently stroke and comfort Joel, to soothe him. What ran fierce and hot moments before still lingered, a sweet time to cherish. Fiona remembered Una's journals, how she spoke of her chieftain, and recognized the tenderness as her own.

To finish the circle, an unlikely love of the battlemaiden will come calling, bearing his angry dragon on one arm and the chest to win her heart. Then the magic circle will be as true as their love.

Joel stirred restlessly, bracing his arm beside her head. He picked a leaf from her hair, smoothing it. His expression was so tender she could have cried. She *was* crying.

Joel's tenderness slid into disgust, his fingers stroking her damp cheek. "I hurt you again," he stated flatly.

She stroked the back of his neck, following the taut muscles, and shook her head. "No. You didn't hurt me. I was thinking of how lovely this is, so beautiful it makes me happy."

He closed his eyes and shivered. "Lovely. We've just dropped our jeans and had each other."

She nibbled on his bottom lip. "Well, there was all that beautiful, steamy kissing. Is your bottom cold?" she asked, patting it fondly.

"I can't practice tonight," Fiona told Joel on Thursday morning when he called to order roses for Mamie. "Tomorrow I've got two baby showers, one huge bridal shower and paperwork to do for two upcoming weddings, and poor Mr. Wailey passed away. Everyone is sending flowers to the funeral—that's tomorrow morning. I've got to stay at the shop tonight. You understand, don't you? We did practice last night and you're very good. We can fake it."

Joel gripped the telephone tightly. After making love to Fiona on Tuesday and Wednesday nights, he wasn't giving her up to flower arrangements. "I was never good at faking," he said, realizing how formal and businesslike he sounded.

He'd called Cody earlier, attempting to soften their relationship, and he'd wanted to hear his son's voice. Cody's belligerence had raised walls, and Joel had sounded hard as his son had tested him. Joel realized how much he had to learn about parenting and Fiona Tallchief.

Damn. He realized he was hurt, dismissed for her job and flowers. He understood rush deadlines, heavy workloads and business demands. He understood the ache in him that Fiona's absence created. "I could help," he offered, not expecting her to accept.

Cradling the receiver to his shoulder, Joel wiped grease from his hands. They were big and not made for delicate flower stems or handling a woman gently.

After a hesitation, Fiona returned, "Joel, I really don't think so. I took several courses on arrangements, and this spring I placed in several contests. It is more difficult than it looks."

He glanced at the old chain saw that he had found, loved, and had promptly disassembled on the floor. His tools were in neat order, as was his habit. He nudged his favorite wrench with his foot, tilting it. After a sharp conversation with Cody, who was still furious with him, and not at all enticed by having a horse, Joel had counted on holding Fiona in his arms.

She fit him perfectly.

But when it came to flower arrangements, he was in the way. Joel glanced at the old sewing room and the potted red jasmine plant. While Fiona was making love, her wildflower scent had slid into heady frangipani. The red jasmine plant reminded him of the blood upon her sheet and how he had taken her innocence. Unused to needing anyone but himself, Joel now needed to see Fiona. "Have you eaten?"

"Just a bite. I've been busy," she said over the sounds of snipping and running water.

During their lovemaking, she hadn't whispered endearments or encouragements to him. Fiona had been too busy exploring the riveting sexual drive and her own body's reaction.

Joel should have given her something...some gentle words scraped from deep inside his emotions, bits of tenderness that a woman could cherish from her first time. But he'd been silent, locked in the fierce, driving heat and the hunger. He didn't know if he knew how to be intimate at such a time, or that he could serve romantic endearments when needed. Damn it. He wanted Fiona to have tenderness to remember, not bruises on her wrist. Complimenting her on her performance wouldn't do, not when she'd given him such an intimate, lovely gift to treasure.

"I'll pick up something and come over." Joel opened his refrigerator door to study the casseroles in it. The single ladies and the mothers of unwed daughters had kept him well supplied. He selected a pasta and salmon dish, topped with cheese.

A half hour later he rang Fiona's back-door, after-hours buzzer, the heated casserole wrapped in a towel in his other hand. Tina Turner's steamy music vibrated through the greenhouse. Fiona hurried through the dimly lit greenhouse, wearing an apron over her sweater and jeans. She unlocked the door, and reached out to grab the casserole with one hand. She whipped off the towel, bent to sniff the food appreciatively and closed her eyes as if already tasting it. She slipped her arm around his neck and drew him down for a quick kiss. "Mmm. Food. I haven't had time to eat since last night. I love you, my prince."

While she hurried away, bearing her prize, Joel blinked. Fiona had shocked him once again. An "I love you" was no small thing to him. His background, even with Mamie, did not contain hugging or displaying affection. Joel, Rafe and Nick had learned at an early age that hugging and telling each other they loved was a symptom of male weakness.

My prince. The words embraced him cozily. Joel let himself in and locked the door behind him. He considered the potted rows of fuchsia-colored hydrangeas. On the other hand, "I love you" from a Tallchief was a serious matter. He ran the flat of his hand over the heather starts that were bound for the Tallchiefs' parents on the mountain.

Abe—or George—sprang from a lacy fern onto the back of his hand. The lizard angled his head sharply. His beady eyes blinked as though greeting Joel with a smile. George—or Abe—whipped around the tile on the floor, leaped onto Joel's jeans and hurried upward on his leg. Minnie twined around his legs. "Hi, everybody," he murmured with a grin that came deep down from inside his heart. "Daddy's home."

"Mmmft." In the shop, Fiona took the fork from her mouth and stuck it into the casserole, devouring it. Amid a clutter of bows, greenery, huge tubs of flowers and the various gladiolus stuck in her apron's big chest pocket, Fiona seemed like an oversize, lean and sexy elf. A pink baby carnation had been tucked over her right ear and a blue one over her left ear. A huge ribbon circled her head, the bow resting on her crown. She pointed to a chair cluttered with paper, indicating that Joel should sit down.

Taking care not to hurt Abe and George, Joel eased off his leather jacket. Fiona glanced at him, stuffed the fork into the casserole again and lifted it to her mouth.

Joel stiffened and then slowly opened his lips, allowing Fiona to feed him. The new experience and the intimacy of the act shocked him. He realized how little experience he had with considerate women; he'd chosen his previous associations to equal his uncomplicated, structured life.

"Mmmf?" she asked, asking if he liked the food, a smile on her lips.

"Mmm," he murmured, agreeing that it was good...good to be cared about, good to be appreciated and good to be her prince.

In her stride, Fiona hummed Tina Turner's "Proud Mary" and added gyrations and fancy footwork as she moved, whirling between flowers, bows and ceramic pots. While Fiona snipped bows and stuffed stems into a ceramic bootie filled with green, damp foam, Joel tried to make sense of her notes and ordering system. Apparently Fiona had her own business systems and none of them organized or legible. She hurried past him, stopped and raised on tiptoe to kiss him.

Joel folded his hands together and waited as she hurried off, down into the nursery to return with a huge potted hydrangea. She stopped, studied the calla lilies in the tub at her feet and muttered, "I'll never get all this done. Poor Mrs. Wailey...poor Mr. Wailey. He was just ninety-five—"

She glanced at Joel, tears brimming in her eyes, and with a bouquet of red carnations between them, came to stand against him, her head on his shoulder. The gesture was so trusting and needing that it startled Joel. He slowly, carefully enfolded her in his arms. She leaned closer, snuggling to him and he swallowed, unused to the emotions circling him. He gently placed his cheek along hers and opened himself to the wave of tenderness.

She sniffed once, and he took a tissue from the box to hold to her nose. "Blow."

Fiona looked at him, her lashes damp from tears. "You would have liked Mr. Wailey. He was the best small-motor man around. I learned a lot from him. Mrs. Wailey won't know what to do without a putterer around. Everyone will have to reclaim all their lawnmowers, washers and whatever he wasn't able to repair."

Unused to sharing himself, or comforting, Joel struggled to say the right thing. He cleared his throat. "I'll visit Mrs. Wailey and see if I can help. Meanwhile, there are babies coming into the world. There are ceramic booties and bassinets to stuff with flowers. I think Mr. Wailey might like that, don't you?''

She rested against him again as if he were her anchor in a stormy sea, and Joel stroked her back. Comforting Fiona felt right; he realized that he had offered little comfort in his life and that it was awkward for him. Yet he intended to try—Fiona looked tired and sad. "Is there anything I can do to help you tonight?"

She sighed tiredly and arched against Joel's hands as he massaged her tight shoulders. "I've done the funeral things. You know, he never said anything about my arrow he found in the sheriff's garden tractor. I was really rather good with a bow, though I never killed anything. I couldn't.... There are just the centerpieces for the showers—forty of them."

"Lead me to them," Joel murmured, pushing back his sleeves. He couldn't wait to get his hands on the flowers. "What's the theme? Round? Square? Or one of those Japanese designs with a stalk here and one there?"

Around the daisy stalk between her teeth, Fiona mumbled, "I don't know about you helping me with arrangements, Joel. This isn't as easy as it looks."

Fiona studied herself in her apartment mirror. Joel's flower arrangements were strictly linear, arranged in a row and all having equal heights. He seemed so pleased with himself that Fiona couldn't bear to correct them while he was there. She'd artfully added different layers after he'd gone out the door whistling Bach.

She'd delivered the arrangements to the appropriate places and found Joel speaking quietly to Mrs. Wailey at the funeral. When she'd come to his side, he'd taken her hand, holding it.

The first Friday night in November found her fearing her first real date with a potential suitor...a candidate who terrified her and made no effort to hide his attraction for her.

Fiona angled her head to one side and adjusted the huge red silk bloom above her ear. The last few nights practicing the tango with Joel always led to contact, sooner or later, and an immediate desire to have him.

Fiona removed the red flower and drew Una's blue beaded necklace around her throat. She tied it, running her fingers over the three strands, sky blue beads against her neck. She wasn't prepared to feel so feminine with Joel.

She was terrified and shy of this first real date with him. She'd been to proms and dated other men, but more for the event than the male she needed at her side. Fiona turned her back to the full-length mirror and looked over her shoulder to study the simple black dress with tiny straps and a thigh-high, fringed hem.

Joel was to pick her up at the apartment; he'd insisted. Fiona had the odd, sinking feeling that this set a new standard, a landmark, in their relationship.

Her hand trembled as she smoothed the short skirt, and the longer lace dance pants beneath it. The strapped heels completed the Latin American look.

She heard Joel's pickup crunch in the alley behind her greenhouse; she clicked the switch to unlock the back of her greenhouse door for him.

Fiona brushed her fingertips across her lips. She'd never tried to be feminine, appealing to a man. She'd never played he-she games—except in the line of duty, a rescue or a cause—she'd never...she'd never cared this deeply, or allowed herself to. If Joel didn't react so marvelously to her, she wouldn't be so excited by him.

He would want structure—life run on a calendar, proper etiquette and table settings, with dinner at a regular time.

Fiona knew she couldn't live her life by a tidy checklist. She held her breath as Joel's footsteps came up the stairway to her apartment. "This is no good," she muttered. "Tangoing with Joel, entering this contest is as good as telling everyone that we're...we're seriously involved."

She opened the door, and beneath the hallway light, Joel stood dressed in a high-collared black silk shirt and flowing pants. His dressy black shoes gleamed. She slowly looked all the way back up to his chest and studied it. "Suspenders. Scarlet ones. How perfect."

When Fiona's father wore suspenders, something always lit in her mother's eyes. Once her mother had whispered to Fiona, "You can never go wrong when a man is careful about his suspenders, dear."

She loved Joel in suspenders. She loved him in nothing at all.

Fiona shivered. A relationship, one with P's and Q's and crossed T's, with Joel wouldn't do.

"Just an impulse," Joel stated tightly, defensively, as if she'd tease him.

"You're perfect," she whispered, her throat drying as she ran her fingers up and down the suspenders and tugged them lightly. Her mother had been right. Joel in black silk was one thing, but the suspenders added just the right sense of excitement.

She shivered slightly, awareness streaking under her skin. Joel had the look she'd seen on her brothers' faces—that male predator look when they wanted to claim their ladyloves. Fiona wasn't certain she wanted to be claimed, or restricted. Joel looked too dominant, too male, too...

"Are you shy of me?" he asked softly, trailing a finger down her cheek. "I thought we'd passed that."

"You know very well this is different. It's so formal." She threw out her hand. "It's like serious dating. This is not like me going to your house or you coming here, Joel...this is dating. Dating means courtship. Courtship means— Well, it used to mean—"

His eyebrows went up, questioning her. She floundered. She wasn't all that modern when it came to Joel.

"Don't be nervous of me, Princess. I thought you were the bold one who liked uncharted waters. Formal dating might not be so bad."

"Oh, sure, for you. People will talk. They'll start marrying us and the first thing you know—"

Joel sighed dramatically and shook his head. "Some people are just prone to logic. I think you're beautiful tonight."

He edged aside the long fringes to view the lace dance pants. "Only you could pull off an outfit like that. You are an exciting woman, Tallchief."

She backed into the room as he handed her a flat box wrapped in a huge red bow. "What's this?"

She dove into the wrapping, tearing it apart while Minnie swatted the bow. The silken shawl, complete with fringes and huge scarlet flowers spilled into her hands. Joel swept it around her shoulders, adjusting the folds. "A little present. Would you wear it for me tonight?" he added formally and kissed her bare shoulder.

Fiona's body moving smoothly, elegantly against his, was a dream. They could move through life, just like this, he decided confidently as they were announced the winners. Because he felt wonderful, elated, floating, Joel couldn't think of a better way to celebrate than to give Fiona a Valentino kiss, bending her over his arm.

He grinned when she straightened and blinked up at him. "Now that was impulsive, Joel. Palladin's Iron Man is slipping."

"You betcha," he tossed back as Maddy announced the talent contest.

"Tangos assume that the male is dominant and that the world is his," Fiona stated very softly. "But I think you need to know, Palladin, that keeping up with me won't be easy."

Forty minutes later, after Sally Jo Black had sung a husky, sensual rhythm and blues, Pete Spade had clattered his spoons to music, Ellie Mae White had twirled her baton, an Elvis impersonator had gyrated, and Mo Bookman had chimed his bells, Maddy announced, "Everyone here has listened to Miss Fiona Tallchief sing for years. She's got three songs tonight, then the tango contest. Give her a hand, folks."

Joel settled back in the shadows, leaning against the bar. He wasn't certain how he liked Fiona singing for other people...still it was charity, he reminded himself. The four-man band tuned up, and Fiona moved onto the stage. Fiona had been shocked when she'd discovered that they were in a structured courtship pattern; Joel would have to analyze the situation. Maybe he was moving too fast; maybe he wasn't romantic enough. Maybe his flower designs showed too little promise and imagination. Catching a butterfly wasn't that easy.

Living separately wouldn't do. He couldn't sleep and he worried about her.

He'd never shared himself with anyone. His intimacy with Fiona seemed to come naturally, because he wanted her to know what made him tick. It only seemed honest.

Joel frowned. There was always that element of his father's legacy. Could he trust himself?

Fiona adjusted the microphone to her level; Joel settled deeper into his thoughts. While she was singing "Greensleeves," he'd decide how to ask her for their next date. He hadn't asked her yet, and he wanted Fiona to have everything, including proper invitations—women should have something to remember...little dance programs to put in their diaries, bits of flowers and little love notes. He would start making a list of appropriate romantic phrases and words and practice them.

From the stage, Fiona studied him coolly, assessingly.

Joel shifted uneasily. Accustomed to business memos, he'd have to practice love notes and study perfumes. No perfumes, he added a second later. He preferred her natural scent like wildflowers on the mountain.

The kiss to her bare shoulder had been an impulse and one he would repeat.

The heady rhythm began, and Fiona started moving slowly, sensuously, doing nothing more than clicking her fingers to the guitar's beat. Her eyes locked with Joel's. He sat up as she began Tina Turner's "Steamy Windows." With appropriate steamy moves, Fiona leaned back and let the raw sensuality pour from her.

The men in the room were instantly taut, even Mel Jensen, who had just reached his hundredth birthday. Joel pinpointed three males he knew had dated Fiona briefly. They were in her past, while he was in her future.

He coolly surveyed the room and his gaze shot back to the three men again, whose eyes were slitted, locked to Fiona's gyrations.

But she wasn't focusing on them, directing the song to Joel.

He relaxed slightly, then shivered, his body hardening and his senses telling him that Fiona was very carefully explaining to him that he was too conventional for her rebellious lifestyle. Joel inhaled sharply. Or she was making it clear to the audience that she was merely having a fling with him. He definitely was not a "fling man."

Hips swaying, fringes flying, arms lifted and feet braced wide on the stage, Fiona launched into the sensual rusty-toned beat of "What's Love Got To Do With It?"

Then to shock him further, she began a sexy introduction into "Addicted to Love." He knew exactly what she was doing— pointing out to him that she wouldn't be the conventional mate, conforming to his corporate standards: Tina Turner and Bach wouldn't mix. Joel recognized the addiction-to-love symptoms instantly—they were his own.

By the time the beat was heavy and Fiona was damp with sweat, Joel had enough. He grabbed their coats, strode through the audience, held them up to Fiona and said, "Hold these."

When she reached for them, he grabbed her wrist and pulled her over his shoulder. He began carrying his woman to a more private place, where she could issue all the challenges she liked. While she squirmed and threatened him, he tugged down a handful of fringes to cover her dance pants, whipped the shawl over her backside and blew a clinging fringe from his cheek.

The three Tallchief brothers immediately launched to their feet, only to be pushed back by their respective and laughing wives.

Joel dumped Fiona in his pickup, watched her gather her temper to tell him where to fly and reached for her. He spared her nothing of his desire for her, his hands keeping her close as his mouth fused to hers, slanted and dived deeper.

"There. Is that what you wanted?" he asked, shaking with desire as she stared at him.

"Not quite." Fiona looped her arms around his neck and drew his lips to hers. Her tongue flicked at his lips, her teeth nibbled around his jaw.

He began to shake, realizing that he wanted her badly enough to haul her over him—*right on Amen Flats' main street!* He'd carried her off over his shoulder like a macho, arrogant male. Joel blinked. With Fiona, he did feel proprietary, unique and up to breaking his personal rules.

"What was that about?" he asked unevenly, trying to recover from Fiona's sensual suckling of his earlobe.

"You looked too smug," she whispered smugly. "You sat there, leaning back with your arms crossed. You were frowning, concentrating on just how to handle the situation, plotting, and confident that you would succeed. Your expression said you had everything under control and it was purring along nicely in the direction you had intended. You reminded me of Palladin's Iron Man, the first time I saw you sitting behind your desk—scratch, scratching at notes, looking cool, efficient and complete, without anyone in your life. The temptation was just too much—I had to do it.''

He had to ask. "Was all that for me, Tina?"

Fiona placed her hands along his cheeks and kissed him softly, tenderly. She plucked his suspender strap gently. "Just for you, my prince.''

Nine

Fiona dragged the cold mountain air into her lungs. Morning Star, a descendant of Tallchief's stallion, moved through the one-inch blanket of snow, easing upward on the familiar trail leading to Fiona's parents' meadow.

October was over and November and hard winter were beginning. Restless with her thoughts after Joel had left her at two o'clock, Fiona had left before dawn. This could be the last chance she had to visit her parents on Tallchief Mountain before winter prevented it. In the spring, Fiona would come with Elspeth to plant the heather starts, while their brothers and Alek cleaned the small meadow of broken limbs.

Joel. *Joel, you frighten me.*

Was the legend true? Did circles complete?

To finish the circle, an unlikely love of the battlemaiden will come calling, bearing his angry dragon on one arm and the chest to win her heart. Then the magic circle will be as true as their love.

Magic. If there was magic, why had her parents died? Why

wasn't her mother weaving and holding her grandchildren upon her lap and her father talking about cattle and lambing and—

Fiona shivered, memories chilling her. Yesterdays were gone, yet through her ran a solid thread, woven into her life and Joel's. A man battling against his dark legacy, Joel wanted more for his son.

Fiona studied the familiar trail. The nearby meadow was covered by a light blanket of snow; the meadows and rocks of Tallchief Mountain had reminded Una of Scotland. While he was staked out for torture, Liam, son of Una and Tallchief, had first met Elizabeth. To save her sister from the lawless gang, the English lady had bowed to their tormenting demands and had later married Liam. Their love had grown.

Then high on those rocks, LaBelle had been chased by Jake Tallchief. LaBelle, a world-class jewel thief and matador, had married and desperately loved the dirt-poor, tough Westerner.

Pauline and Matthew Tallchief, Fiona's parents, had been deeply in love throughout their marriage.

Fiona tugged down her knitted cap against the chill. Each of Una's legends had come true, her brothers and sister happily married.

Joel had entered her life only a month ago, when October came to haunt the Tallchiefs with the death of their parents. Now October was gone, and her reckoning with Joel had sliced through the threads of her life.

Tallchief Mountain was bred into Fiona: the jutting rock cliffs, the forests and meadows and the tumbling streams that led into Tallchief Lake.

She reached the small, lush, meadow, where wildflowers would grow in the summer and birds would feed upon the berry bushes surrounding it.

Mom? Dad? Oh, how I miss you.

She dismounted and stood at the small iron fence, slowly opening the door. A leaf flew to her cheek, caressed it. *Mom?*

Fiona cleared away the broken limbs covering her parents' resting place. "It wasn't Joel's fault that he wasn't here that day, Mom. Joel and his brothers came to pay their respects, and I ran them off. They looked so tired and hungry, threadbare city boys on horses they couldn't ride, and determined to pay their respects. They were trying to build pride in themselves, in doing the right thing, and I wouldn't let them.''

She crouched, placing her forehead on her knee, grieving for the circle that had not been completed, her parents' lives cut short.

Fiona carefully arranged carnations and roses and greenery over her parents, the icy wind already tearing at the petals, darkening and tugging them away.

Morning Star nickered, and suddenly a larger hand reached down to hers, easing away a waiting bouquet of daisies. ''Let me help,'' Joel murmured, kneeling at her side.

He removed his Western hat, the wind catching in his hair. Dante, his gelding, sheltered in a stand of fir and pine.

Fiona dashed away a tear that had begun freezing on her cheek. Joel, unshaven and dressed as a Westerner, in jeans and a shearling coat, had followed her up the treacherous trail used only by her family. ''I miss them,'' she said simply.

''I know. You thought they'd be there for you when you grew up, and they weren't.''

She studied him, a man who had not had a childhood or loving parents, who had built his life free of his father. ''I'm sorry,'' she whispered, placing her glove along his cheek.

Joel's expression tightened, his body tense. ''You've got that backward. I should be saying—''

''No, you shouldn't. You've paid enough. Do you believe in magic?''

Joel stared up at the jutting mountain. ''Sometimes,'' he admitted reluctantly. ''It's a new item on my study menu. I think it began when I walked into Eunice's back end. An elephant isn't what you'd expect in a barn. Or maybe it was when I was knocked silly by those cans at the convenience store, and you stood over me, looking like a regal goddess deciding my fate. I thought you were wearing diamonds instead of glass shards.''

''I've never believed in magic—at least for me. I believed in reality and what I could change. There's more to this than the passion between us. I don't know that I want more, because I'm happy now and everything is moving too quickly.'' What was she saying? She had always hurled through her life and now she wanted to carefully examine her relationship with Joel.

"True," he admitted slowly, and Fiona's heart began beating again.

When Joel stood, Fiona took his outstretched hand. He brought the back of her gloved hand to his lips and kissed it reverently.

"Don't, Joel. Don't for a minute think that you owe or need to apologize to anyone because of your father. My parents would want you to be happy...to raise your son here. My brothers and family feel the same."

"Thank you," he murmured so humbly that a piece of her heart tore slowly, painfully.

"What runs between you and I is different...." Fiona considered the clouds sweeping low and close to the mountain. "We'd better get back. Night on the mountain is cold, city boy."

"I don't think we need to hurry," Joel said slowly, placing his hat low on his head and tugging up his leather gloves. He braced himself against the wind, his long legs a distance apart on the thin layer of snow.

Fiona brushed a few fat snowflakes from her eyelashes. "Joel, I was raised here. My family is bred to track and to survive in the wilderness. You aren't."

Emerald bright, his eyes cut down to her. "Aren't I? So, you're protecting me, is that right? You always protect the people that you cherish, don't you?"

Fiona didn't like the deep edge to his voice, challenging her. "Be practical. When snow sets in here, it will probably only get deeper. I wasn't planning to stay, Joel...just to talk with my parents one last time before hard winter closes Tallchief Mountain."

"I *am* planning to stay. There's a stream and a beautiful little meadow just a little down the trail. I left my pack mule there."

"Joel. Think—" Fiona inhaled as Joel swept her into his arms and carried her to his horse, placing her in the saddle. After taking Morning Star's reins, Joel swung up behind her. The move was proprietorial male. She noted the sheathed rifle, a high-powered killer, and reliable protection against the predatory wildlife on Tallchief Mountain. The Tallchiefs liked their wolves, bears, and pumas—at a distance.

She sat very straight, aware of how well Joel managed his gelding. "You've learned how to ride, city boy."

"I've never liked being deficient in anything," he returned too softly.

She took it one step further. "So I assume that Palladin, Inc. purchased cattle ranches for your education and exclusive use."

"That wouldn't have been wise—until Nick, Rafe and I spent a summer on one. After we picked her up and left her in a tree after an argument, Mamie packed us up and dumped us on a ranch filled with hardcase cowboys who adored her. We learned respect with a capital *R* and lots of sweat. Mamie was determined not to protect us as she had my father. If we committed an infringement, we had to pay for it."

Fiona laughed outright, snowflakes sweeping across her face. "You could have run away at anytime, right? Only she had challenged you, and you were determined to stick it out. That's exactly what my family did to me."

Joel glanced at a covey of quail scurrying beneath the bushes, foraging for food. "Mmm. Something like that. The first night we came home after blowing our paychecks at the local tavern—we were all under drinking age—we were building fences at dawn and breaking horses and moving woodpiles. Because I was the oldest and should have known better, I got two woodpiles, big ones."

"And then you bought a ranch, right? A nice big corporate spread with fancy cattle and fancier horses?" She leaned back into the solid wall of his body, enjoying the safety and warmth. An independent woman, she'd scoffed at leaning against a man, and now when she was too weary, it seemed almost like coming home.

"No. First I worked my way through college." Joel placed his chin over her head, gathering her closer, and Fiona settled into the emotion that always surprised her; with Joel, she felt cherished and feminine.

Joel eased the gelding off the trail and into the small meadow, the snowflakes fattening and tumbling across it. He swung down from the horse and held up his hands for Fiona. "It makes a nice hobby for Rafe...Nick is too busy flying, looking for something

I guess we all want. Mamie likes an occasional outing, all very civilized of course. My grandmother likes her comforts, and more than one complicated merger has been sorted out at the ranch, free from interference. Just what don't you like about a formal dating structure?''

Fiona allowed him to lift her to the ground. "With you, it could be very formal. For one thing, there's the way you put your hand low on the back of my waist, as if guiding me when we're entering or leaving a doorway. I've never liked guidance. I've had my fair share from my brothers and sister. Then, there's that pulling-out-chair thing. It obliges a woman to sit, when she might not be considering it."

"I do not guide women," Joel stated tightly. "I like the feel of you beneath my hand—you're very feminine—I can stop that, if it bothers you...and Mamie would have my hide if I didn't pull out your chair," he admitted roughly.

"I'll think about your let-me-take-care-of-you guidance. Your hands are very gentle and secure. Mamie really must be something to manage you three."

"We're docile...now." Joel's tone said that Mamie's taming job hadn't been easy.

She followed him to where the pack mule stood waiting. "I see you know how to pack a mule. That is an art and takes time. Exactly why did you—oh, I suppose you wanted to come by yourself, to finish what I stopped those years ago."

Joel slanted a dark look at her. "You weren't where you were supposed to be early this morning, Princess. I called. Morning Star was missing. October has passed, a hard month for the Tallchiefs' emotions. Logic led me to think you were riding up here. I decided to follow. One never knows when a well-packed mule can be an advantage."

"I often come here by myself. I'm quite safe." Fiona frowned. She felt like she owed Joel an apology. She didn't.

"But you're not alone. That's the point, dear heart. We have a neat little one-to-one relationship simmering on the front burner." Joel took a hatchet and began hacking limbs to form a shelter. He tossed a rope over a sapling and dragged the top down, then another and whipped them together, forming an arc. Fiona had seen the process to make a one-sided shed, protection for the horses against the bitter cold wind.

"You think I owe you an explanation of my daily schedule?" She helped drag the branches, and Joel propped them against the sapling arc, forming a lean-to.

"Yes," he said after a long moment. "Especially when you could be in danger. A snowstorm is predicted. We have a date tonight. You might not have been back in time to make it. I really like those burgers at that little drive-in with you sitting next to me. I was counting on a big Saturday night at Maddy's—several very close dances and a really nice good-night kiss."

She stared at him. "You packed a mule and came all this way because you were afraid I'd break a date?"

"A date is a very important landmark in a relationship. It would not bode well, if we didn't connect. A misunderstanding could result, then another, and an infinite mess could develop. I wouldn't like that. I'd prefer that you know my exact position on our relationship, step by step." Joel's look said he wasn't explaining further.

Fiona decided not to pursue his logic. It sounded too...logical and committed.

When the lean-to was finished, she dusted her leather gloves. "Okay, now that it's done, I'll be on my way. If you're not down in a reasonable length of time, and the weather worsens, we'll come after you."

"Stay put," Joel ordered as he placed the flat of his hand on her chest and pushed her back into the lean-to, tossing a down sleeping bag at her.

Fiona narrowed her eyes. "I spent my teenage years with brothers shoving me around. I didn't like it then, but we were playing for high stakes. Now I don't have a family to worry about keeping safe, so don't push me—"

The sight of Joel whipping out a lightweight chain saw and stroking it lovingly with his glove, stopped her. He placed a kiss on his glove and touched the chain saw before starting it. He revved it up, cut several tall saplings and set about trimming the branches from them in quick efficient cuts.

The wind carried his deep voice to her as he spoke to the chain saw, "You're a beautiful, exciting lover, fitting me just right, and though you're a little difficult at times, I love you. I'd like you to share my life. We'll grow old together."

He revved the chain saw again. "I respect every beautiful molecule of you. I won't leave you or treat you poorly. Trust me. I'll keep all of your perfect parts humming and oiled on a regular basis, baby."

"My, my, how interesting. He speaks to his small-motor repair projects," Fiona murmured, fascinated as Joel formed the poles into the framework of a tepee. She decided to settle down and watch this new man unfold, shrugging off Palladin's Iron Man corporate image.

When the tepee was completed, secured and heavy canvas covered it, Joel began gathering firewood. Unused to being pampered, Fiona worked at his side.

"Well, well, well," she murmured an hour later, when the horses and mule had been given grain, and Joel was frying thick ham slices in a skillet over a properly laid cooking fire. She sprawled onto the thick down sleeping bag and studied him. "Why?" she asked simply.

Joel added a package of hash browns to the skillet, then flopped the cooked ham slices over the potatoes. He tested the hot water kettle braced on the flat cooking rocks with his hand, jerking it away from the heat. Then he added more hot coals to the top of the cast-iron Dutch oven, in which were biscuits. "You're always running so fast—or we're too occupied in overdrive, physical needs. I don't know what pleasures you, Princess. I'd like to know. I'd like to please you."

The simple statement rocked her. "I...I think you're doing fine. You can be quite...impressive."

His grin was quick and devastating, his new beard glossy and black in the firelight. "Good." He frowned, turning his attention to the sizzling potatoes. "The problem is—between you and me—that our discovery time has been too short. We haven't had time to adapt to the surprise."

"Really?" she asked, inviting him on. "What surprise?"

"The magic one." He produced her favorite tea, an herbal

mixture, also her mother's favorite, and tossed a small amount in the heated kettle to steep.

Blast, Fiona cursed mentally, waiting for him to make a mistake; he'd been far too perfect. Couldn't he toss her just one small goof?

"Do you think it's wrong that I want Cody with me, away from everything he knows?"

Joel cared deeply about his son. He drew into himself, his frown indicating that he was afraid of losing Cody, when the relationship hadn't begun. He was sharing an intricate, meaningful part of his life with her, which she appreciated.

"You're doing the right thing, Joel," Fiona murmured, wanting to help him. "According to the postman, you've ordered a ton of books. I would suppose that an amount of them are parenting books, correct?"

He stiffened as though caught doing something suspect. "I like to study situations, circle them, apply new techniques."

"Like now?" Fiona took the cup of tea he handed her. She sipped it and cradled it in her hands as she looked over the top of it. "This is heavenly. You've gone to a lot of trouble, Joel. Palladin, Inc. probably owns a top sporting goods store. In fact—" she lifted the sleeping bag to find the Palladin label "—in fact, you've gone to a lot of effort, when Palladin, Inc. probably has some little uptown, easy to construct, high-tech camping tent."

"I'm showing off," he said as he handed her a plate heaped with food. "The traditional male proving that he can provide what the female should have. It's ritualistic, primitive behavior, but something that I feel—impulsively feel—that I must do for you alone, as my woman...as a matter of pride."

"Palladin pride, correct? And I'm supposed to understand this. I understand perfectly. In the past few years, I've watched the courtships of my entire family. The 'my woman' part is drastic, ringing of possession, and I'm not certain about that. I'm the last, you know. An endangered species—the baby of the Tallchief clan." She dove hungrily into the food.

"The spoiled baby," Joel said too softly and began to eat. His statement hung over the campfire.

Fiona put her plate aside; the hot water wasn't the only thing simmering. "What do you mean?"

Joel continued to eat methodically, his fork loaded exactly the same, as though he were loading his thoughts in the same manner. Then he placed his plate aside, took hers and prepared to leave. "You worried your family. I had quite the little job persuading them to let me come up here, instead of them. You've worried them for years."

Fiona blinked as his harsh words slammed into her. She followed him out of the tepee. "Just exactly what do you mean, Joel? Why are you here? Are you taking up where they left off, protecting me, defining the rules? I don't need to act perfect now, Joel. There's nothing at risk."

"Isn't there? Let me explain this way." Joel tossed the plates aside, swept Fiona into his arms, and when she resisted, they went down in the snow.

His mouth was hot and hungry and yet sweet and cherishing, their breaths mingling in the cold air. Desire slammed into Fiona, her arms locking around him as he rolled over her until she rested on top of him.

She dived into the heat of him, desire lashing at her, and suddenly Joel jerked away, his eyes blazing emerald green. He shuddered, eased away from her and stood to his feet, holding out his hand for her.

"This is my first attempt at making myself appealing and trying to be impulsive for a woman, Fiona the fiery," he whispered quietly, the snow lashing between them as she stood. "I do not want you to forget me, or to discover that I was not up to par as a romantic partner."

In that instant she knew how he had convinced her brothers to let him come after her. Joel had declared his intention; her brothers had understood. Elspeth was probably baking cookies to soothe them as they mourned their loss and cuddled their babies. Her husband, Alek, was probably reliving his battles with her brothers.

Fiona turned slowly to the tepee while Joel placed his arms around her from the back. "This is—"

He kissed her cheek. "My variation of the Tallchief bridal

tepee. You should have magic and dreams, Princess. This is not a temporary fascination for me, and I'm sorting through how to handle a volatile woman who rebels at the slightest logic or imagined restriction. On the other hand, I'd like the courtship part, because I've found that I'm delicate about tradition. I'd prefer not to rush through this interim in your usual style, but focus on intimacy, learning about each other—''

''I know,'' she whispered, leaning back against him and placing his hand over her breast. As the cold fierce wind swept around them, Fiona knew that for this moment, her heart's circle was complete. ''Love me,'' she whispered.

Joel checked on the horses, bracing the branches securely around the lean-to, and collected more wood for the fire. He wanted no distractions from what he considered his wedding night. He glanced at the tepee, sheltered in the pines. Fiona had taken her time walking to it, as if at anytime, she would choose to leave.

For a man who commanded boardroom discussions and difficult mergers, who made rules for others to obey, the prospect that this level of their relationship might fail terrified Joel. He'd keep his reference to commitment light, keep his emotions intact, and would be certain not to hurt her.

Night had closed in on Tallchief Mountain, and when he entered the tepee, Joel's body reacted instantly to the sight of Fiona waiting for him, firelight warming her bare arms and shoulders. His hands trembled as he secured the flap. Fiona's scent curled up to him, mixed with wood smoke and the pines outside. One thing at a time, he reminded himself, as his body hardened into a painful ache. He stripped away his gloves and coat and rubbed his stubble-covered jaw. ''I'll shave.''

''I could do that for you,'' she offered.

''Not tonight. Thank you.'' One touch, one look at Fiona's body and— Despite the cold, he took his time, and his taut emotions caused a razor nick. He washed with soap and warm water that Fiona had just used and he withdrew fresh towels from the pack and placed them nearby.

"Come to bed, Joel," she whispered, shocking him. "That is, if you're done planning how to handle me."

Wearing his silk shorts, Joel eased into the sleeping bag, "I should have warmed this for you."

"Joel. I was raised on camping trips. I wrapped hot rocks and placed them inside the bag before I got in." Her breast brushed his arm, the soft warmth surprising him. "Mmm. This is nice. I like the wind and the cold outside and you inside."

Fiona moved over him, bending to nibble on his jaw. "You look so serious, as if you're thinking what to say, preparing a verbal brief. You might as well get it out."

Her hips bumped him intimately, and Joel's body lurched, immediately coming into contact with her moist heat. As always, Fiona was moving too swiftly, and soon he'd be too far gone in passion to think.

Joel turned her easily, resting over her. "I want to make very certain that you remember this night, Princess. I want to take it slow and easy, and I have things to say."

Her eyebrows shot up. "But you've been very silent."

"I've decided you need variety." He placed his hand upon her breast, caressing the softness. "You are not exactly talkative during lovemaking, either."

"Mmm. Making love. That has such a nice sound to it." Fiona's hands smoothed his back, caressed his bottom and moved up to his chest. She tugged at the waistband of his shorts. "We're going to talk? Now?"

"I thought I'd lead, and we'd take it from there. Think of it as a tango, just to get started." He glanced down at her hands, pale in the firelight, and toying with the hair on his chest. He brushed his thumb across her nipple and noted the quickening of her breath, the arch of her body, flowing beneath him. Joel kissed her shoulder and nipped her earlobe, almost groaning when her breasts slid against his chest.

"Joel?" Fiona breathed rapidly, her mouth raised eagerly for his.

Joel eased aside and while Fiona looked at him, her eyes steaming and her body trembling, he ran his hand down the length of her body, caressing her. He ran his thumb along her hipbone and splayed his open hand over her stomach, thinking of a child that might one day nestle there, if there was truly magic in his life. The muscles in her thighs contracted as he tasted them lightly, moving on to her stomach, flattening his hand against her, sliding his fingers lower to stroke that moist intimate warmth.

Fiona shuddered. "You're going to be difficult about this, aren't you? It's so much easier to just take what we want."

Joel lowered his head to suckle one uptilted breast, and then he lay beside her, shoulders and hips touching, his hand smoothing her gently. "I like lust. Good old-fashioned, honest lust with a physical woman, namely you. I desire you from the time I wake up in the morning until I can manage whatever sleep during the night. When I'm inside you—"

His fingers slid along her body, cherishing the curve of her hips, the indentation of her waist. "How do you feel when I'm inside you?"

She sucked in her breath, shivering and grasping his shoulder as he bent slightly over her, to better see her expression. Fiona did not hide her desire—her eyes smoky and heated beneath her black lashes, her mouth moist and trembling, her color high. "Do we have to talk?" she asked, and Joel smiled at her slightly frustrated tone.

"It would be a first, if we can manage it."

"You think I can't manage a conversation now?" she asked in a tone that said she'd picked up his challenge.

"I want to be desired, sweetheart. I want to laminate myself to you, feel your heat as my own, taste your mouth, move in you. I want to taste you down one side and up the other." Using the images that Fiona had given him when they first shared a bed, Joel continued, "I want heat and storms and thunder, bodies slick and bursting, twisting, breathing like one."

Joel turned Fiona on her stomach and kissed a line across her shoulders and down her spine. She groaned and shivered as his hand swept down and then up to rub gently between her legs.

"This isn't fair," Fiona gasped as Joel nuzzled her neck and eased her to her side, facing him.

"Tell me about how you feel. Now. Right now."

Fiona's open mouth raised to his, her tongue flicking his. "You're wanting a lot."

"I want foreplay, during play and after play. I want to fill you, and keep filling you, and draw out, and fill you again."

"I want to hold you tight inside me, against me." Fiona's hands skimmed down his chest, and Joel sucked in his stomach as they stopped.

He closed his eyes, body throbbing, aching, then relented, sliding off his shorts. "Take me inside you, and we'll continue."

Her lips curled against his. "You won't be able to talk then, my prince."

Yet her hands curved around him, encircled him and gently examined him. "I told you once that I wanted no easy lover, Palladin, and you've been much too gentle, fearing to hurt me. If we're going to be honest, I'd prefer that you forgot everything but me. *Tell me what you want from me.*"

Her hips undulated against him, the sensual friction almost taking him. Joel forced his body to still, because tonight, Fiona was not leaping from A to Z. Her untutored hands were exploring him intimately, and he could sense his body tilting dangerously into lack of control.

In a gesture Joel decided was heroic, he reached out, dipped his hand in the bucket of cold drinking water and dashed it on his face.

Fiona laughed, delighted. "You won't make it, Joel."

"Won't I?"

He drew her knee over his thigh, cupping her buttocks and caressing them. He began to speak softly, smoothing Fiona's breasts, her back, her legs. "We haven't begun, you and I. You're right, I've been very conventional, careful not to shock you. But—" Joel eased slightly inside Fiona's warmth and felt her heat pour over him. He closed his eyes and slipped deeper, her uneven sigh coming as a deep-throated purr.

"When I'm inside you, I think how I'm the only man you've cared about enough to give your body. I think of how sweet you were that first time, and how—"

"How?" Fiona was breathing rapidly, her body flowing beneath his, opening. Joel eased over Fiona, fighting the rigid desire that threatened to rule him. "Princess, I've never been so deep."

She clasped him tighter. "Don't you dare stop, Joel Palladin."

"How do you feel now?" he asked, desperate for her.

"As if you've always been a part of me." Her hands smoothed back his hair, and the first rocketing contraction sped through her, gloriously amazing to Joel. Fighting his own needs, he waited, rigid, until she came back to him.

He gave her a soft, lingering kiss, and Fiona went wonderfully boneless in his arms. Joel rubbed her nose with his. "Let's talk."

She groaned unsteadily and closed her eyes as he began the sensual friction again, whispering huskily into her ear. "Fiona. You're a part of me and I'm a part of you. I'm deep inside. In another minute I'll be giving you myself, and from that could come a child. How do you feel about that?"

Through her passion, Fiona stared at him, her fingers digging into him. "Joel?"

Then her expression changed, a fierce demand adding to her emotions as her hand swept lower and Joel shuddered, almost losing control. "I want everything. I want it raw and true and good, straight from what you feel," Fiona whispered against his lips, then suckled his tongue as her hips rose to meet his. "If you try that blasted control and logic, I'll know, and I won't have it, not with you. Not now."

Despite her demand, Joel managed to control his body. Just. He feared hurting her. Another fierce wave hit Fiona, and her teeth sank gently into his shoulder, her cry muffled against his skin. "Come to me," she whispered fiercely as another wave hit her.

Passion hit Joel broadside. He arched, easing deeper, deeper, and fought the heated pressure devouring him. He raised her knees for the first time in their lovemaking, and Fiona gasped with the deeper invasion, then hurled herself hungrily against him.

He forgot to be tender. He forgot control. Joel dived into the fire, her body pulling at his, her helpless tones driving him on. At the height, fighting for release, Fiona cried out, bolting high as Joel touched her intimately.

She took him closer, their skins blending, heating, becoming one, bodies locked, pitting themselves against the inevitable. A strong woman, Fiona demanded, and Joel gave. He demanded, bringing her hips up tight against him, suckling her breasts, and Fiona ignited.

The pounding heat swept them away, lingered, pounded again, and flung them into a pulsating world where only he and she existed. Joel tried for control, and instead laced his fingers with Fiona's, his kiss desperate as he poured himself into her.

Heartbeats later, while Joel was trying to summon strength to lift his head from her breasts, Fiona smoothed his hair. "That was not ordinary, everyday sex to feed basic needs, was it?"

Joel smothered the smile touching his lips and eased up to draw her close to him. He kissed the black, glossy head resting on his shoulder. "Nope. Not even close to basic, average lust."

Her hand smoothed his stomach. "You gave me everything, didn't you?"

"Everything. We had no ordinary loving. I'm afraid...I'm afraid I was too rough."

She groaned and curled around him, stroking the dragon on his arm. "I think you're marvelous. I like how you make love, soft and gentle, or raw and open and truthful, as if you're giving me the best part of you."

Long after Fiona lay sleeping in his arms, Joel stared at the firelight shadows on the tepee. *Did he want too much?*

Hungry for her again, Joel eased Fiona to her side, cradled her breasts and kissed her shoulder. She arched back against him and inhaled as Joel entered her moist warmth.

Fiona looked down at Joel, sleeping innocently. He'd had her again, softly, gently, awakening her with encouragement— "So sweet, Princess. You're so soft and warm and—" He'd paused as he had eased gently inside her. She would remember that fullness forever, the gentle way he held her.

"Tell me," she'd whispered in the darkness, her hand pressing his against her breasts.

"That you're all I want? All that I've ever wanted?" he'd asked unevenly, gathering her close against him. "That when I see you, a part of me feels like I'm wallowing in peaceful sunshine, where the world is right and happy...and the other part starts heating and thinking of ways to have you?''

His gentle rhythm had seduced, intrigued, his words flowing urgently around her. ''You give me so much, making me a part of your life and now a part of your body.''

The heated waves had come gently firmly upon her, and again Joel had given her his unique gift.

Now, looking down at Joel sleeping beside her. Fiona realized that Joel probably had never revealed himself to another woman. That he'd saved that portion of his life for her and that though words were difficult, he wanted to give them to her.

She eased her hand to his stomach, smoothed the slightly hairy surface and circled his naval with her finger. Joel groaned unevenly, arching to her touch, and his arousal rose gently to her stroking.

Fiona came upon him, settled and made their bodies one. He awoke slowly, wonderfully, powerfully, this man she'd claimed. She took him as fiercely as the night before, and hoped to shock him thoroughly, for he had stepped inside her heart and had frightened her.

Again he poured into her, giving his essence, his life to her—not a light matter for Joel Palladin, who guarded himself well.

With the wind howling around the tepee, Fiona settled at his side. Joel's dark green eyes were drowsy, his expression pleased and dreamy. ''Let's make this legal,'' he whispered. ''Then you can take me every night.''

She looked up at him. ''Joel, you don't think this could be—''

''Love? Could be. I haven't got any experience with what we're going through now, but I know it's good. You make me feel good just being with you or thinking about you.... Go to sleep, Princess.''

''But you want harmony and structure in your life. I can't give you that. I don't know if this is wise, talking while we're making love, or after it.''

''We're relating, sweetheart. Becoming more intimate than physical need can take us. We're communicating.'' Joel patted her bare bottom and added drowsily, "You give me more than harmony and structure ever could."

Fiona slipped from Joel's arms to add wood to the fire and to bathe. Joel had been careful to lay out lush towels and feminine soap. There were advantages to having a logical prepared man nearby. She knelt by the fire, aching in places deep and private and recently shared by Joel. Fiona realized that she joined other women who had given themselves completely and then had risen to cleanse; a private, feminine moment to contemplate the past hours. Thinking of Una and Tallchief and the chest's legend, which had entered her life, she soaped her face, breasts and arms, and stood, facing away from Joel, to complete the rest of her body.

Emotion ran deep and true between them after the loving. Physical needs had eased into gentler ones, truer, enduring ones. Joel looked at her like her father had looked at her mother: as if nothing else, no one else, mattered. As if she were his treasure.

He was no easy man, ridden by the past. Yet he'd torn away his familiar control and had given her the truest part of his heart. For Joel, he'd broken his own rules for her, no easy matter.

His hand circled her ankle, the dragon on his arm flexing as she looked down. "Turn," he requested softly.

Fiona lifted her head. A private woman, who kept her secrets, Joel was asking to look at her body. Her lover had not seen all of her body in their lovemaking, and she was shy of him now.

He had given all of himself, tearing away from the past, from what he feared, and she could do no less. Fiona turned, holding the towel against her, then dropped it slowly.

Joel stroked her ankle, his dark gaze flowing slowly upward, filling her with a heavy gentle warmth. When his eyes locked with hers, Fiona said what was in her heart, "I will never forget this time with you. I will never hurry so fast through life, that you—this won't be a part of me. You will always be mine, Joel Palladin, because I have chosen you."

Ten

While the washer began the rinse cycle, Joel slipped the broccoli and chicken casserole into the new oven and checked the dinner rolls rising beneath a damp cloth. The romaine lettuce had been rinsed and waited in the refrigerator for salad. The table had been set with candles and place settings. Joel frowned and eased a dinner fork noticeably askew. He slipped the cookbook he'd been using back onto the shelf with the other new ones and glanced out the kitchen window. The middle of November hung in layers of cold damp mist, and the Tallchiefs had invited him to Thanksgiving dinner next week.

Dante and Morning Star were in the big pasture, and a small milk cow, a gift from Duncan and Sybil, was in the corral, getting used to her new home.

In the barn was Joel's brand-new shop, a small neat room with wide, well-lit work counters and strong shelves. He had several new projects from Mrs. Wailey, and he didn't want his home to look like a garage. He wanted his home to look intimate and comfortable for the woman who would return to him that night and lie in his arms. He ran his hand over the bouquet Fiona had brought him last night, treasuring it.

She'd let him help her replace the spark plugs in her battered, beloved Jeep, and the task had seemed a very intimate sharing, especially when they ended up on the bales of hay, making love.

He tensed, reminded of how he had tried to think, to give her those nice sweet words that he felt, but sometimes they came with difficulty, especially when Fiona was in a hurry. Her hit-and-run tactics left him stunned and frustrated, because he wanted her to move into his home, share it with him. He hadn't asked, because Fiona was a woman who would choose her time.

An independent woman, Fiona had been mildly surprised as he'd laundered, cooked and cleaned. Joel shrugged, dismissing any potential comments from Rafe and Nick. So he liked making a home for his woman, so what? When they found a woman they wanted to cook for, he would loan them a cookbook.

Joel slipped the dish towel from his suspenders and hung it on the rack. House husbandry was a relaxing pleasure, but he spent every morning after Fiona left tending to Mamie's business needs and his personal financial accounts. The rest of the day was his, to scrape free the old linoleum in the bathroom, to tinker with his motors and to plan the addition to his home.

Cody's bedroom was waiting, not the high-tech one he would expect. His son's computer escapades would be highly limited and monitored by Joel, replaced by stacking firewood and a regular round of chores.

What did he know about being a father? About knowing when to give and when to set down rules?

He studied the overstuffed easy chair he'd had reupholstered, rough beige fabric replacing the huge cabbage blooms. Mix and Match slept in it, overlapping heads and paws and snuggling together. The adjustable standing lamp stood nearby, and a wooden bookshelf that needed refinishing was laden with seed magazines.

Joel ran his hand down his jaw, testing the smoothness of his late-day shave. He wanted his relationship with Fiona on a firmer basis before Cody arrived. His son's defiance rose a notch with every passing day. At times, the two most important people in his life were the most frustrating ones. Joel wanted both of them to know exactly how he felt and what dreams he hoped for in their relationship.

Dreams. He'd had them from the first moment he'd held his son, and from the moment Fiona stood over him, "diamonds" glittering on her shoulders. He hadn't known that goddesses could be so rebellious or volatile or passionate, giving him more than— He closed his eyes and saw her again in the tepee's firelight, standing tall and straight and feminine.

Fiona's Jeep sailed down the road and screeched to a stop in front of his house. Joel usually stood on the front porch, for the sheer pleasure of watching her come home to him. But today he moved into the shadows of the old sewing room, watching her. Today, he wanted her to come to him, to admire the fine old wood furniture he'd found, to see it in the light of the sewing room, surrounded by her plants. She frowned, glancing at the porch, then took carrots to Morning Star and Dante, petting and talking to them. Long legged, dressed in jeans, boots and a warm woolen jacket, Fiona resembled the "boy" Joel had first met at the convenience store. Always in a hurry, she strode to the little cow and patted her through the fence.

Joel liked Fiona patting his backside; it made him feel appreciated. She was his first experience in many ways.

Fiona glanced at the house and frowned. Joel settled deeper into the shadows. She would have to come after him, because he had a surprise for her. He loved giving her gifts. Her pleasure was absolutely genuine and feminine, like a wild rose unfolding—

Fiona burst through the door. "Joel? Are you here?"

"In here." He reached up to slightly unscrew a lightbulb; he didn't want technology cutting into this magical moment.

"What are you doing?" she asked, moving into the shadowy sewing room. She clicked the light switch. "Joel, you need a new bulb."

"Okay. I'm arranging furniture. What do you think?"

Fiona whipped off her knit cap and stopped as Joel eased her coat from her, tossing it to an old bench beneath the windows. "What...?"

She stopped, staring at the old pioneer loom that occupied one-third of the room. Fiona circled it, and outside, a soft rain began to trail down the window, creating moving shadows within the sewing room.

"I missed you, Princess," Joel stated simply, filling his senses with her scent, her slow pleasure, as she studied his gift.

Fiona turned suddenly and absently kissed his cheek. "Oh, hello, honey."

Joel swallowed tightly. Fiona had just given him an endearment. He floated a little off the floor.

She frowned at him. "Joel? Do you weave?"

"Nope. Not a strand. There's too much organization, structure and logic involved. It's yours. I thought you might enjoy it when the snow is deep and—"

She hurled herself into his arms and placed her face against his throat, her body shaking. "Hold me."

He held her close, terrified that she would refuse what he offered. "Are you going to cry?"

"I'm thinking about it." She turned to the loom. "I...thank you."

Joel smoothed her hair, combing it with his fingers as his heart kicked up two beats and leveled into a firm, hard race. Joel smiled into her hair, nuzzling the soft, glossy texture. Tempting Fiona was the best game yet. "You don't think the room is too full? That some of the furniture should go into another room?"

Fiona moved away from him, scanning the shadowy room. "Not really. But if you think so, we could move the potted plants and—"

She looked down at the small wooden cradle her boot had just touched and crouched beside it. Joel held his breath as she traced Tallchief's man and woman stick figures.

Fiona's fingers reverently skimmed the handcrafted wood. "Duncan and Sybil have the original one in which Tallchief and Una placed their babies. Calum, Birk and Elspeth have ones that Tallchief made and sold to support their family. This must be one of his—"

"It was in the barn with the loom. Someone had taken care to protect them against damage, and I merely cleaned them. They are yours, Fiona."

She placed her forehead on her knee and rocked her body.

"You're making this very difficult, Joel. But you intend that, don't you?"

"I want you to remember me. Is that bad?" Joel lifted her into his arms and kissed her damp cheek.

Fiona turned closer to him, wrapping her arms around him. "Joel—"

He gently nudged her cheek, asking for her mouth; he had to tell her with his kiss how much he adored her. She opened her lips to his seeking kiss, and when her arms tightened and her body pressed urgently against his, Joel lost himself in the simmering heat.

He held Fiona tightly, hoping he could make it to the bedroom, because the couch was definitely closer—

Over Fiona's soft, hungry purrs, the rain began pounding the windows, the primitive rhythm matching their passion. Recognizing the unwelcome slam of a car door, Joel tried to pull back.

She arched up against him, hungry now and trembling, Joel tried to ease her away as the footsteps crossed the wooden porch....

Cody, Joel's ten-year-old son, jerked open the front door and stood, glaring at Joel who held Fiona in his arms. Rafe pushed Cody, dressed in a ball cap, an oversize coat, and jeans and battered sneakers, into the room and closed the door behind them. "Mamie thought sooner was better," Rafe explained wryly.

"Sooner is better. Hello, son." Joel wanted his son, and the woman in his arms. Joel held Fiona very tightly before lowering her feet to the floor. She turned to Rafe and Cody and trembled, her fingers digging into his shoulders. Then as if they had not been locked in passion, she slid from his arms. Joel latched his hand on to the back of her neck; she wasn't running from him now, not when he had the two mismatched edges of his life in the same room. As Cody glared at them, Joel had the distinct sense that his world was hurling into the dirt.

"This place is a cabin, not a house," Cody stated, glancing around the living room.

"It's a lovely home with lots of love circling it. You must be Cody. I'm Fiona Tallchief," Fiona said easily. "Take off your coat. Joel has supper waiting for you."

"He didn't know we were coming. That was the only condition to me coming here—that no one tell him. My uncles and Grandma do not break their words," Cody shot back at her.

While Joel dealt with his aching, unfulfilled body and the unexpected arrival of his furious son, Fiona seemed unaffected, moving easily into welcoming the new arrivals. "I'll take your coats. You look just like Joel. Which one are you? Rafe? Nick?"

Joel studied her. She moved away too easily from him, dismissing what had just flared between them. He wasn't happy. One last, longing glance over her shoulder would have soothed him.

"Rafe. The best of the lot." Rafe shrugged out of his jacket and grinned at Joel. "Nice suspenders. Looks like all that cooking has made your face a little hot."

Joel would take care of his brother later. He looped his hand around Fiona's wrist. She wasn't leaving him.

"I hate this place," Cody muttered.

A small hot-pink four-wheeler pulled into the ranch yard, and Fiona grinned. "That's Emily delivering Sybil's best berry pie. You're in for a treat after dinner, Cody."

"Yeah, right. I don't want to be here. I want to be with my friends in Denver."

"Uh-huh. Maybe Emily will stay for dinner. You look just like your dad and uncle, and they are handsome men." Fiona held Joel's hand as though she knew how badly he wanted to say the right things, how badly he wanted to hold his son.

"I hate girls—"

"Girls can be difficult, but this one is special. She's Fiona's niece." When Joel opened the door, Emily hurried into the house, a redhead dressed in a cobalt blue sweater and long leggy jeans with Western boots. Cody stared openmouthed at her. When introductions had gone around, he was still staring at her and apparently unable to speak. When dinner was finished, Cody's eyes hadn't left Emily, who seemed quite happy with his attention. "I came over to ask Aunt Fiona if she could help me with my archery bow. It's the old kind, a straight wood bow, and Dad says she was always the best archer around."

Over his ice cream and berry pie, Cody turned slowly to Fiona and blinked. Joel knew exactly how his son was feeling—fascinated by the Tallchief women. "Fiona can handle an eighteen-wheeler with the best of them, too."

"My kind of woman," Rafe stated with a grin and stood. "Sorry I can't wash the dishes, old man, but I've got a date in Denver. Cody, I'll bring in your things. Joel, his school records are on the way for his enrollment here, just as you asked."

Joel studied his son. His backup plan of a private tutor wouldn't be necessary. Cody had refocused back on Emily, who said, "I'd love to see your room. I'll help you unload, okay? And listen, if you need help adjusting, or catching up on homework or anything, you know—making the change to a new school—you'll let me help, won't you?"

Cody cleared his throat and made what Joel considered to be a valiant effort for a stunned male. He straightened, edging for more height near Emily, who was taller. "I'd like that. You say Fiona can handle a bow? Well, I've been thinking that I'd like to learn how to handle one of those. Not the high-powered, compound kind, but the old-fashioned ones."

Emily winked. "Fiona and Elspeth ride like all the Tallchief women. You should see them. I'm learning, too. We have a fall rodeo, and skiing and sledding in the winter, and hay rides. When I first came here, I didn't like it, because I didn't know anyone, but you know me already, and Fiona. The Tallchiefs are a great family. You'll feel just like one of them in no time."

Joel smiled at Rafe, who had just winked. "Women," they both said, appreciating the opposite sex.

"You'll be just fine, honey," Fiona murmured before leaving. As they stood beside her Jeep, she lifted on tiptoe to kiss his cheek and snapped his suspender playfully.

Joel caught her hand and brought it to his lips. "I like it when you call me 'honey.' I'll phone you later tonight."

She kissed his lips and whispered, "You're doing everything right, Joel."

"Not quite, or you'd be in my bed tonight," he returned tightly, and flicked her lips with his tongue, needing a more intimate taste of her.

Her smoky look made him want her immediately. He cupped

the back of her head with one hand, raising her lips to his deep penetrating kiss, and caught her close with his other arm. "Remember that," Joel murmured, satisfied, as Fiona blinked and stared at him, her slightly swollen lips parted.

"You just asked for it, my prince," she threatened in a husky purr as she revved up the Jeep and roared down the farm road.

"You bet I did, and I plan for it to include a wedding ring," Joel said quietly as he turned back to the house and saw his son watching out the window. He motioned Cody to come outside, and when his son stood nearer, Joel lightly put his hand on his shoulder. "Come out to the barn. I'd like to show you something I'm working on. Maybe you can help."

Cody stiffened, moving away from his father. He glanced painfully up at Joel. "Just don't try the buddy stuff, okay?"

Joel inhaled and studied his son's determined scowl, which looked so much like his and his brother's. "You look like me, you know."

"Yeah. So what?"

"Well, maybe we like the same things. We'll just have to find out, won't we?" *Give me a chance, son. I'll try my best to make a life for us. I love you.*

"Motors! All kinds of 'em," Cody exclaimed with delight a moment later. "My dad is a motor fiend! Have you ever souped up a racing cart?"

"I don't get it. Why don't they all just go to a restaurant or something. It's too much work and mess," Cody muttered a week later, the evening before Thanksgiving dinner. At the Tallchief ranch, the kitchen was bustling, the Tallchief women baking bread and pies and crumbling dried bread for stuffing while their husbands were home tending babies.

While they discussed what he should plant in the spring, Joel was helping Duncan with Megan and Daniel, both of whom did not want to go to sleep. Duncan had been summoned into the kitchen to unscrew, lift and fetch. Cody tried to remain a safe distance from the children. "Crawlers everywhere," he muttered, as Megan plopped herself in his lap, showing him her dolly.

"They are a family who like being together, especially on holidays.'' Joel rocked Daniel, whose big gray eyes were getting heavy. He'd missed so much with his son. "When you were a baby, I wanted to rock you."

"I didn't need it," Cody snapped, easing away from Megan.

"You did. So did I."

"You scared me. You always looked so hard and mad. You look different now. But I'm leaving, just as soon as—'' Cody stared at Emily who had just breezed into the room after a ball game. The long-legged, teenage redhead ripped off her coat, tossed it aside, and with an unconscious feminine movement, shook free her long hair. She picked up Megan and hugged her.

Cody looked as if he'd been hit between the eyes—stunned and gaping at Emily. Joel knew exactly how he felt.

"Hi, guys. Hi, Cody. Sorry, I'm late. I'll go help in the kitchen right now. How's school?" She kissed Megan.

"Just great. I like it here. Can I help cook?" Cody asked, staring unblinkingly at Emily.

"Sure. Here," Emily said, and eased Megan into his arms. "Let's go into the kitchen and see what we can find to eat first. I build a terrific sandwich. I'm starved."

"Great," Cody said, and, taking a deep breath for courage, kissed Megan's cheek.

Later, riding home in Joel's pickup, Cody asked, "Why did you chase Fiona, Dad? I mean, you're awfully old to be running after a woman who's just snapped your suspenders, aren't you? And why did you look so—you had this silly, proud expression on your face when she clipped your hair. I don't get it."

"Fiona makes me feel good, son. She's a part of my life, just like you are." Joel wasn't that relaxed; he craved one little "honey" from Fiona, who would be sleeping alone in her bed tonight. He stopped his groan, longing for her.

Cody looked out into the night, the moonlight outlining a deer beside the road. "The Tallchiefs are wearing kilts tomorrow. The guys, too. What kind of a family does stuff like that? You won't ever catch me wearing nutsy stuff like that. People can see right up to your— And what's the deal with the scars on their thumbs? And all that 'Aye' stuff?"

Joel tried to organize how to tell his son about the Tallchiefs' parents, and who was responsible. "Cody, a long time ago, a man shot their parents. There were five of them and they were just teenagers," he began slowly.

When the story was done, Cody settled in to think, and Joel recognized the familiar brooding expression. "Okay," Cody said when they got home.

"Okay?" Joel asked, uncertain about the simple agreement.

"I'm okay with all this. I'll try." He looked at Joel. "The thing is, Dad, you're a little impulsive sometimes now, and I'm not certain how I feel about my dad patching my pants or shirts."

"I used to do that for your uncles. I guess I missed doing it."

"Hard times?"

Joel nodded, and Cody continued to look out into the night, his young face serious. "You really want me, don't you?" he asked after a long moment. "You want me enough to leave everything you know and come up here, where you are an outsider. I remember your office and your suits and how you knew what you were doing. Here, you're reading lots of books just to find out what to plant. It must be like going back to school."

"I really do want you. I love you, son."

"Mom said you didn't. She said you were always too busy for me."

Joel ached for his son. He needed to hold Cody, to keep him safe, but Cody was wary of him. "I was very busy, and I tried to see you. But I didn't think I was the better parent...because of my father. Your mother's parents are great."

"There's stuff people don't see," Cody muttered after a while. "It's all like a great big picture you have to put on for everybody, to make everything look good, when it isn't."

"That isn't going to happen with me, Cody. I promise."

Cody looked at him. "Fiona is your girl, isn't she? Where does that leave me?"

Cody was too old and worn for his age; Joel chose his words carefully. "That leaves you with me, no matter what. But I'd like Fiona to be my wife. I'd like you to have brothers and sisters. I'd like us to be happy. Together."

While Cody digested Joel's statement, his father mentally repeated Una's legend: *Then the magic circle will be as true as their love.* Was the completion of his life too much to ask? Was there an outside chance that Fiona loved him and that Cody could be happy?

"Fiona gave me an old top. It was in the chest you gave her. She said she wanted me to have something special from her great-great-grandmother, isn't that something? Rafe has a top collection, but nothing neat as this. It looks crummy, but it has perfect balance and spins like a—" Cody grinned. "A top. Are you in love with Fiona?"

"I am. But I want her to have what all women should have, a time to cherish before settling into marriage. I thought six months would be enough time. What do you think?"

"I think you need to watch the soap operas. Those guys whisk right in there and sweep a woman off her feet, and it's mush before you know it. You don't seem to be doing so well."

Fiona listened to Joel's footsteps moving up her stairway to her apartment. It was December now, a storm brewing on the mountains. Cody was in Denver, visiting his uncles and grandmother during school break.

Joel was being very careful, determined to relate to Cody, and sometimes the task was not easy. Joel wanted harmony in his life, and Fiona respected that and knew his need for structure.

She smiled, snuggling into her bed. Life with Joel in it was pure delicious excitement. An unexpected boyish grin could take her heart spinning; one look could find them locked in passion.

Joel opened her apartment door, closed it, and she listened to the sounds of him packing away groceries in the kitchen. So. Palladin's Iron Man wanted to cook breakfast, did he? Fiona smiled as the carpet muffled his footsteps on his way to her bedroom.

He stood at the door, outlined—a big, broad-shouldered man, still uncertain of their intimacy, of what to say and when, of handling her. He found her in the darkness and relaxed slightly. When he undressed, Fiona marveled at the powerful, lean line of his back, his hip, his thigh.

He came to her, needing her, and she opened her arms, taking him. She smiled against his shoulder as he began, "Sweetheart, let me look at you...just let me look at you."

While Joel had a weekend planned with her, scheduling it carefully between breakfast in bed, visiting with the other Tallchiefs and taking her out to dinner and dancing—and probably happily repairing the noisy motor on her refrigerated display window—she fully intended to demolish his harmony and ravish him. Joel was the best, most excitement in her lifetime, and so delightful when caught unaware.

Yet there was peace in her now, an unexpected bonus to this new level of intimacy with Joel.

She glanced at Una's chest as Joel's trembling hands found her. *Then the magic circle will be as true as their love.* With Joel moving over her, desperate for her, his body heating, she did believe in magic and love. They'd started so fast, unaware that intimacy would come with and after the passion. Would it last?

"Lovely, just lovely. He's been missing for a week, and now he's in the hospital, and not a word to me." Fiona crushed the Denver newspaper in her fist. Joel's face had been urgent as he'd mediated a standoff between the police and a desperate man. According to the headline, Joel was the only person who had influence over and the respect of the troubled man, who had already shot one policeman.

"Joel and Cody have been missing for the past week, and not a word from him. My brothers knew it, they had to, and Alek, as the editor of the newspaper had to have known." Furious with Joel, Fiona whipped out of her shop, leaped into her Jeep and roared off toward Tallchief Lake.

Pride had not let her call after the first few attempts. She wouldn't have Joel on a platter. She'd worried, hadn't slept and had ached for him.

She geared down for a curve, eased over a small bank of snow and onto the pristine snow of the road. Christmas had been beautiful, but now Joel had shredded that lovely peace.

Fiona dashed away the tears burning her eyes. Without explanation to her, he'd packed up Cody and disappeared. So much for trust. So much for legends of love.

On the snow the Jeep angled, slid and lost traction, coming to rest gently against a tree. Fiona stepped into the cold mist and ran to the lake where the Tallchiefs had pledged to stay together. *"Aye!"* She could still hear their voices raised to the night storm.

Was her heart tearing? Why hadn't Joel called? Hadn't he needed her just as desperately as she needed him?

She dashed aside a snow-laden branch. Fine. She'd had her physical needs satisfied, so did he. What about the tenderness snaring her deeper with each day?

She'd gotten what she'd wanted—lust. Nothing more, or less. She could cope...live without Joel and the magic that had just begun. Couldn't she?

Joel grimaced as the fresh wound tore slightly in his shoulder. Though bandaged and treated, the healing flesh did not like Joel's guiding Dante down the road to Tallchief Lake. He'd wanted to come to her before the story broke in the newspapers.

"Damn." Joel noted the Jeep on the slight incline, resting against the tree. If Fiona was hurt—

He saw her at the edge of the fierce, wind-swept lake, white-caps tossing furiously on the black water, night creeping down the mountains. Joel let Dante pick his way through the trees, finding the old horse trail in the snow. He held his breath as Fiona pivoted, facing him, her body taut as though preparing for battle.

"What are you doing here?" Fiona demanded rawly, wrapping her arms around herself and bracing her legs apart.

Joel dismounted, his breath hissing as, beneath the bandages, the wound tore again. He walked slowly to her, the snow drifting between them. This was the woman he loved, that he would always love, and she felt betrayed. "You're cold. I brought your Tallchief plaid. Here, take it, you're freezing."

Oh, she'd been crying; he'd hurt her.

Fiona grabbed the plaid as if not wanting him to have any part of her life, and pain slammed into Joel, worse than the new bullet wound in his shoulder.

She swirled the Tallchief plaid around her and looked off into the lake, her head high. "Leave me."

He could no more leave her than stop breathing. Joel moved

behind her, longing to bury his face in those soft, black, wind-tossed strands, desperate to hold her and know that she was safe.

Fiona pivoted, turning on him, her gray eyes misting with tears. "We set out to have each other, didn't we? We've done that quite thoroughly and now—"

"I love you," Joel stated, his heart racing. He couldn't bear to hear her say that their love was over. "I'll always love you."

Fiona trembled and gathered the plaid closer to her, the wind whipping at it. "Aye and blast, you do, Joel Palladin. That was no loving man who ran off without a word."

Anger ran through her, her words slicing him like a hot sword. She tilted her head, slanting him a look. "First I lost my parents, and I was so angry with them for leaving me. I understand that is a natural reaction. Then you came into my life and I found— for a time—peace. Peace, Joel. Do you know how rare that is in my life? Absolute, utter peace and an excitement that tugs me into the next day? The freedom to leap upon you and have you, to tell you things I've kept secret all these years? My fears? What was your plan? To structure a seduction, and gain my trust, and then destroy it? Was this all a game to you, built with careful, methodical little blocks that you could rip away? Do you know that I actually began to like the security of your schedules? Is that what Palladin pride is? To seduce and to hurt?"

Joel battled her jarring thrust and the weave of nausea passing through him. The doctor had prescribed rest, but Fiona was more important than Joel's life.

He tossed his pride aside. "I was afraid for Cody. Paul Sims had just lost his son, and in his twisted mind he thought I shouldn't have had a healthy one. Sims lost total control in Denver, and I had to act fast. He respected me at one time—and I understand his grief about his son's fatal illness."

Fiona's head went back. "You could have told me, or called. Not one word in a week, Joel. After a steady diet of sex, I would think you could call."

Sex. The word was cold and hard, slamming into him. "Your brothers thought it was best—and so did I—to keep you out of it. You're not exactly the stay-at-home-and-be-safe kind of woman, and I didn't want you hurt."

Fiona stared at her boots. "I'm supposed to believe this. I'm not helpless, Joel. I would have gone with you. I'm good, really good in a pinch. You're a hoarder still, keeping secrets from me."

Nothing was more important than now, that she believed he loved her. He traced the smooth line of her jaw, set with tension. "I'll always love you, Fiona."

"Aye and blast," she muttered and began to cry. "Why didn't you call? Don't you know that a part of my heart died when I read that newspaper?"

The wound in his shoulder waylaid him, drugs making him imagine Fiona was undressed by the campfire—that she was smiling down at him, that she was safe against him. He cleared his throat, uneasy with his weakness. "There was a small matter of a bullet—"

Fiona's head shot up, steel gray eyes ripping down then up his body. "Where? Where did it hit you? *Why didn't you want me with you?*"

"First question—my shoulder. Second question—I wanted you like hell—"

Fiona's hand sliced across his explanation. "Don't tell me. You walked out of the hospital the minute you could. Which shoulder? I want to know, because I'm going to hit the other one. Oh, Joel, don't you know how precious you are to me?"

"Right shoulder. It's fine." She cared. Joel clung to that *precious* word and wallowed in it. "It's embarrassing," he admitted grimly. "The nurses were calling me 'Romeo' because when I was delirious, I was—"

Joel cleared his throat, feeling his blush move up from his throat. "I thought I was a poet. An erotic one. And the poems were all dedicated to you...and that's the last I want to hear about it."

Fiona looked at him, her expression softening as he dried her tears with the plaid and carefully enfolded her against him. "Because I don't want to hurt you, I'm not going to grab you, but at some point, after you're well, I will. And I'll want every one of those poems, written and tucked in Una's chest for me to cherish." She smoothed his unshaven jaw, brushing her lips against his. "You'll always come for me, won't you, Joel?"

"Always. I love you. I have from the first moment I saw you."

"Aye and blast, then in return and to be fair and honest, I should tell you that I love you, and that magic circles do come true. There will be no more waiting and dating and planning, and handling me so delicately I ache, Joel Palladin. You have your pride and I have mine, and so it will be, because you're not escaping me, my love."

Fiona kissed one cheek and then the other, and while Joel wondered if he was dreaming again, she whispered, "I love you, my prince."

Epilogue

Fiona took her time, combing her hair, arranging the sleek, glossy length over the Tallchief plaid around her shoulders. The first of October had come again, cold winds circling Tallchief Mountain, and she had chosen her time.

She picked up the mirror, lying beside her on the bed she had shared with Joel, her husband, since that January day, because neither would be separated, even for a night. She tensed, glancing at the bedside clock and counting the time between her pains—the baby was as impulsive as she, hurrying to be born a week ahead of schedule.

When she relaxed, saving her strength, Fiona looked at the woman in the mirror: a peaceful woman, glowing with happiness, and one who was well loved by her husband, new stepson and the growing Tallchief family. She'd fought her battles and had come home to find peace.

Home was where her heart had come to rest. Her home was with Joel, the husband who shared her intimate thoughts and gave his back to her, now only slightly uneasy with the sharing.

Una's chest glowed in the bedroom's shadows, as much a part

of her life as the other dowry legends were of her brothers and Elspeth.

Because Joel and Cody were hovering too near, she'd sent them off to collect flowers and plants from the new owner of Hummingbirds. She had other things to grow and tend and love now. Because she could not move to her loom, setting the weave and the world right, Fiona settled for her tatting shuttle, giving herself to the rhythm of making lace.

Fiona gasped, the pain coming stronger.

"Aye," she whispered, her hands smoothing the mound of her stomach. "When your dad comes home, you'll not frighten him. He's plotted and planned for this. He's got my bag packed and waiting for hospital, and he's carrying a list in his pocket, mumbling about it in his sleep. I'm afraid he'll have to toss that one away and follow his backup, this-won't-happen-but list—"

Joel and Cody arrived, slamming doors, hurrying to see her.

His hair tossed by the wind, a grin upon his face and his hand upon Cody's shoulder, Joel entered their bedroom. "Taking a nap, are you, Princess? Look what we've—ah..."

He stared blankly at her. "This is not your due date," he stated firmly as if the baby ought to care for schedules and planning.

"I know— Aye and blast!" Another fierce pain took her—

Joel tossed the flowers aside, whipped off his coat and hurried to her. With her fingers locked to his, loving him, Fiona had to tell him, "Joel, honey. Get your lists and your books, because this baby is not waiting. Cody, call my sister, would you? Elspeth will take care of the rest. They'll want to know. Oh, no, Joel. Don't look so desperate. My family will come, but it is you I want— Oh, and Cody? Please put water in the vases for the flowers, will you? I'd like them here."

"I love you," Joel stated so fiercely that she recognized his fear.

Because she felt another pain, Fiona had no time for gentleness. She reached out to grab his shoulders and tugged him down for a fierce kiss to tell this dear man that she'd love him forever. "Come with me, my love, my dragon. Step into the circle, and I will give you a child."

* * *

Two weeks later, at Ian Palladin's first outing, Fiona looked at her family, gathered at the old Tallchief homestead, where she had been raised, fighting rules and leaping into causes.

Dressed in their kilts and plaids and frilled shirts, and surrounded by their families, the Tallchiefs had come together for a family picture. October winds hurled through the cold night outside, and none would forget that it was on a night like this—With legends and love wrapped around them, they had survived and began new loves and new generations of Tallchiefs.

Calum stopped fussing with the preset timer on the camera and declared the clan hold still. Cody's new puppy yelped from the back porch, demanding attention.

Fiona inhaled and straightened. There was Duncan the defender, Calum the cool, Birk the rogue, and Elspeth the elegant, always dear to her, and their families gathered around them. They had worried over her, protected her, and she loved them desperately. Now they had families and homes, and life had come full circle for her. Una's legends had come true.

Love shone in their expressions, their eyes bright with tears, and none tried to shield their emotions as they looked at her, the baby of the clan, who had found her peace.

Elspeth, her only sister, and the one who had inherited the ability of their Scots-seer and Sioux-shaman ancestors, had a look that said she'd known all along that Joel would come calling one day and that Fiona's legend would come true.

Sybil, Duncan's wife, stood on tiptoe to kiss away the tear on his cheek. Birk, towering over his petite wife, Lacey, looped his arm around her to draw her against him. Calum placed his cheek against Talia's, his expression that of dreams come true.

Cradling Ian against him, his other son dressed in a kilt beside him, Joel held out his hand to her. Against his tartan was the delicate length of tatted lace she'd made to keep him safe during the baby's birth.

He'd fretted and cursed and promised that she would never go through that pain again—but she would—after giving him time to recover from the way his list making went awry. Ian Matthew, like his mother, was a suspect rebel, while Cody marched to a scheduled, planned tune. While Ian had the Tallchiefs' gray eyes and black hair, the tiny cleft in his chin was definitely the mark of a Palladin.

Fiona took her husband's hand and leaned against him, his arm encircling her, holding her close and a part of him as the camera flashed. The circle was complete. Fiona had come home at last. There was magic in legends, and the Palladins' dark, stormy legacy eased more each day...for a proud, honorable man, Joel would have none of it touch his sons or his wife.

"Aye," Fiona whispered softly.

"Aye," the Tallchiefs called together, raising their thumbs high.

"Aye, Princess," Joel murmured, looking down at Fiona, his green eyes filled with love.

High on Tallchief Mountain, a blanket of leaves rustled over the meadow where birds would sing and heather would grow in the spring.

To finish the circle, an unlikely love of the battlemaiden will come calling, bearing his angry dragon on one arm and the chest to win her heart. Then the magic circle will be as true as their love.

* * * * *

THE PALLADINS SERIES *by Cait London*

continues!
Turn the page for an exciting sneak
preview of Rafe Palladin's love story...
coming your way this August,
only from Silhouette Desire.

'Twil be the knight who brings his lady to this cave with clusters of crystals about—aye, the sparkling crystals shall shoot their cloak of colors about him, who loves her already. Rogue that he is, the lady will come to love him with all her heart.

Rafe Palladin's Story

"**A** moat and a closed drawbridge. Just what every castle in Wyoming needs," Rafe Palladin murmured as he stood overlooking the small valley shrouded in snowflakes.

He tugged up the collar of his coat, leaned against his BMW and dropped into his thoughts. Acquiring the castle and therefore soothing the conscience of his grandmother, who felt guilty for her son's crimes, would be an easy task. Mamie Palladin wanted Dr. Valerian well repaid for the folly he had purchased from her son, the small castle that had plunged the Valerians into debt and was sucking Dr. Valerian's health.

Rafe found the small crystal attached to the key ring in his pocket. As a boy, he had discovered it in the same castle, and for some reason he'd kept it as a talisman.

The Valerians, father and daughter, would probably leap at having the castle taken off their hands—and the handsome profit. As chief of Palladin, Inc.'s Acquisitions and Product Development, Rafe had the quick-claim deed in his briefcase, ready to be signed. He'd follow Mamie's orders, though it went against his nature to give money away. Rafe had teethed on darker elements than charity.

He scanned the low clouds, blanketing the mountains and laden with snow. With his grandmother, Mamie, and his brothers, Joel and Nick, Rafe had been trying to set right their father's crimes and scams.

Lloyd Palladin's schemes had ended in a life sentence for murder, and he'd been killed in prison. He'd given his sons nothing, not even pride. They'd built that with Mamie's help. His grandmother had jerked her grandsons from the streets, shoved them into decent clothing, taught them rules and manners, despite their fighting every inch of the way.

Rafe ran his hand through his neatly clipped hair, surprised at the fine trembling. He studied his hands, neatly manicured but big and tough like his father's. Hell, all the Palladin sons looked like Lloyd: dark brown hair, green eyes and a cleft in the center of their chins.

He felt as lonely and out of place as the tiny castle yanked from English soil and hurled, stone by stone, into the Rocky Mountains. The last twenty-four hours had torn Rafe's life apart. His mother's letter, written years earlier, had been sent by a friend of hers, and last week Rafe had discovered that Belinda was not his biological mother.

Joel and Nick were not his full brothers.

Through everything—Belinda's early death, his father's brutality and schemes—all Rafe had ever had was the knowledge that the three Palladin sons were a unit—strong, invincible, building their pride from nothing.

And now, he wasn't one of them.

"Hold. Who goes there?" a man called out as a fresh blast of icy wind whipped around Rafe. Though it was only five o'clock, the cold mountain night shielded the castle now, and Rafe stood in front of his headlights, making his identification easier.

"Rafe Palladin, of Palladin, Inc." Rafe glanced out into the shadows, remembering when his father had brought him and his brothers here, to patch the castle, "pretty it up," to sell it. Joel, Nick and Rafe were too young to do the men's work their father had demanded. He had ridiculed them into doing it, covering rotten boards with new ones, sweeping out the clutter of pack rats, scrubbing the windows. Rafe had been badly cut, too young to use a power saw. To save a doctor bill, Lloyd had cauterized it with a knife's hot steel. So much for tenderness.

At night, while their father drank steadily, the brothers had lain on the floor and dreamed of being knights, protecting the castle and all who lived within. Rafe had held the crystal to the light, lost himself in the myriad of colors bursting from it and dreamed of the princess that he would rescue one day.

Rafe frowned as the drawbridge began to lower, chains creaking. He'd been a part of his father's scam, taking Dr. Valerian's retirement and his savings.

"Enter and welcome. Will you sup with us, friend?" the man asked cheerfully, as the heavy planks of the drawbridge slammed into the ground. "Did you say, 'Palladin'? I bought this wonderful castle from a Palladin."

"I'm his son." Rafe forced the admission. He went back to the car to turn off his headlights and pick up his briefcase. As he made his way across the safe parts of the drawbridge, a rotted board tumbled down into the mote, filled with snow and debris.

"I'm Dr. Nathaniel Valerian. Welcome to my humble home, my castle, so to speak."

"Father!" A women's indignant tone hurtled at them as he opened the door. A woman who barely reached Rafe's chest and wore a circlet of gleaming black braids on top of her head hurried to Nathaniel with a woolen shawl, draping it around his thin shoulders. She drew him into the kitchen. "Father, just look at your feet. How many times have I told you to wear your boots when going out in the snow?" she demanded, then glared at Rafe over the tops of her round glasses as if he were the culprit who had caused Nathaniel to misbehave.

"And who are you?" she demanded in a tone that matched the bitter, freezing weather outside the kitchen.

"My daughter, Demi Tallchief. After her divorce she reclaimed an ancestral name, which has made me very proud. Perhaps you've heard of the Tallchiefs of Amen Flats. We are distant cousins and have recently made their acquaintance. She prefers

Demi to Demeter, who was goddess of the harvest. Are you familiar with Greek mythology, Mr. Palladin?"

"Call me Rafe. I'm afraid I've never had time to study mythology." Rafe saw no reason to chitchat about his own new relatives, the Tallchiefs. In his experience, a business deal was better without charity and friendship. From the way the woman hovered around her father, she was more parent than child. According to Rafe's preacquisition research, Demi was thirty-one and divorced. She would have influence on Valerian's decision to sell the castle, and Rafe would have to find her weaknesses.

"Palladin?" Demi asked, her narrow black eyebrows lifting. Her gray eyes seemed to smoke, narrowing threateningly at Rafe. "The man who wrote the letter, and the acquisitions director of Palladin, Inc.? *The son of the swindler?*"

Rafe turned slowly to her and met her cold stare. A man who battled for his pride, Rafe disliked her accusing glare down her straight nose and over her glasses. The shade of her eyes reminded him briefly of a stormy sky reflected in his crystal. She folded her arms protectively over her chest. "My father said we're not selling, and that is final."

Her voice, though clipped and furious, held softer tones, a feminine husky tone that snagged at Rafe. "I thought a personal visit and discussion might better—"

"No. Since you have no further business here, you may go."

Rafe studied Demi Tallchief. Though she might not be familiar with the "stand and fight" motto of the Tallchiefs, she was not making his visit easy. Demi's eagerness for Rafe to leave only made him more determined to stay. She obviously ruled the castle, and Rafe would enjoy seeing what happened when she was challenged....

* * * * *

*Don't miss Rafe and Demi's love story, coming in
August, only from Silhouette Desire.*

DIANA PALMER
ANN MAJOR
SUSAN MALLERY

MONTANA MAVERICKS Weddings

RETURN TO WHITEHORN

In **April 1998** get ready to catch the bouquet. Join in the excitement as these bestselling authors lead us down the aisle with three heartwarming tales of love and matrimony in Big Sky country.

A very engaged lady is having second thoughts about her intended; a pregnant librarian is wooed by the town bad boy; a cowgirl meets up with her first love. Which Maverick will be the next one to get hitched?

Available in **April 1998**.

Silhouette's beloved **MONTANA MAVERICKS** returns in Special Edition and Harlequin Historicals starting in February 1998, with brand-new stories from your favorite authors.

Round up these great new stories at your favorite retail outlet.

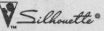

THE TALLCHIEFS

USA Today bestselling author
Cait London continues her beloved
miniseries with

THE SEDUCTION OF FIONA TALLCHIEF
(SD #1135) APRIL 1998

A Palladin man to marry a Tallchief woman? It was unthinkable to anyone in Amen Flats, Wyoming. But April's **Man of the Month,** gorgeous Joel Palladin, has a score to settle with feisty Fiona Tallchief—a score he intends to settle at the altar....

"Cait London is one of the best writers
in contemporary romance today."
—*Affaire de Coeur*

BEVERLY BARTON

Continues the twelve-book series— 36 Hours—in April 1998 with Book Ten

NINE MONTHS

Paige Summers couldn't have been more shocked when she learned that the man with whom she had spent one passionate, stormy night was none other than her arrogant new boss! And just because he was the father of her unborn baby didn't give him the right to claim her as his wife. Especially when he wasn't offering the one thing she wanted: his heart.

For Jared and Paige and *all* the residents of Grand Springs, Colorado, the storm-induced blackout was just the beginning of 36 Hours that changed *everything!* You won't want to miss a single book.

Available at your favorite retail outlet.

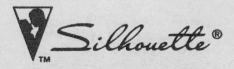

Silhouette Books
is proud to announce the arrival of

A MOTHER'S GIFT

This May, for three women, the perfect Mother's Day gift is mother*hood!* With the help of a lonely child in need of a home and the love of a very special man, these three heroines are about to receive this most precious gift as they surrender their single lives for a future as a family.

Waiting for Mom
by Kathleen Eagle
Nobody's Child
by Emilie Richards
Mother's Day Baby
by Joan Elliott Pickart

Three brand-new, heartwarming stories by three of your favorite authors in one collection—it's the best Mother's Day gift the rest of us could hope for.

Available May 1998 at your favorite retail outlet.